Acclaim for
The Handsomest Man in the World

"In David Leddick's book, *The Handsomest Man in the World*, the narrator meets Fred, the title character, in the South Pacific on a ship monitoring the early tests of hydrogen bombs before coming out was something gay men did publicly. This was a seminal time in history as gay men began waking up to their desires. Leddick has much to say about these early awakenings and does so in some highly inventive flashbacks to affairs with some of America's most famous names.

   This book is not so much written as it is told. One of Leddick's talents is his light touch with a pen. His narrator has an interesting story to tell about his past loves and with that story, the reader gets a great deal of insight into the general nature of attraction and love. In particular, Leddick sheds a gentle knowing light on a part of men's lives that has been lived in shadow. This book recognizes that our sexual urges, when followed, lead us to our more complete selves."

—Tom Bianchi
Author of *On the Couch, Volume 1*

"David Leddick's *The Handsomest Man in the World* is a sexy romp through 1950s America. Reverberating with pained romanticism, the novel captures a spirit of defiance that no longer exists and may no longer be possible—a spirit with a perseverance based on the most tenuous of hopes. Through a poignant juxtaposition of cold-war mentality and the love of two sailors, this novel offers a stunningly genuine sense of what life in mid-twentieth-century America was like for gay men. Suggestive of Isherwood and Baldwin, Leddick's novel sparkles with moments of camp, wit, and pith while proving utterly refreshing in its sense of unaffected sincerity and heartfelt honesty. In an age that celebrates pessimism and irony, this book dares to revive our respect for love."

—Dennis Denisoff, PhD
Author of *The Winter Gardeners*;
Assistant Professor, Ryerson University

"Many of us my know David Leddick for his works about the course of male nude photography across the twentieth century, where he has traced that genre's course of expanding possibilities. In this, his fourth novel, Leddick turns his eye for visual nuance into telling descriptions of the men—particularly the title figure—that his narrator encountered in the fifties, when both Leddick and his narrator were young.

Readers who are old enough to remember the fifties should find his descriptions of the decade's straight-mindedness as apt as his descriptions of life at that time in the Navy, in California, or in New York City. We can easily imagine that his sense of the constraints that came with life aboard a ship or in the cramped rooms and apartments that provide most of the settings in the book flow from his own experiences.

The novel orbits around a bittersweet recognition by the narrator that the one great love of his life left him to marry, have a family, and become a lawyer. Recognizing that his inexperience in sorting out the conflicting claims of sex, romance, love, and social propriety, the narrator—having had several long-term lovers and a successful career as a painter—concludes that he has been blessed with 'all the best of my second choices.' "

—Joseph Marchesani, PhD
Assistant Professor of Integrative Arts,
Penn State University at McKeesport

The Handsomest Man
in the World

HARRINGTON PARK PRESS
Southern Tier Editions
Gay Men's Fiction
Jay Quinn, Executive Editor

This Thing Called Courage: South Boston Stories by J. G. Hayes

Trio Sonata by Juliet Sarkessian

Bear Like Me by Jonathan Cohen

Ambidextrous: The Secret Lives of Children by Felice Picano

Men Who Loved Me by Felice Picano

A House on the Ocean, A House on the Bay by Felice Picano

Goneaway Road by Dale Edgerton

Death Trick: A Murder Mystery by Richard Stevenson

The Concrete Sky by Marshall Moore

Edge by Jeff Mann

Through It Came Bright Colors by Trebor Healey

Elf Child by David M. Pierce

Huddle by Dan Boyle

The Man Pilot by James W. Ridout IV

Shadows of the Night: Queer Tales of the Uncanny and Unusual edited by Greg Herren

Van Allen's Ecstasy by Jim Tushinski

Beyond the Wind by Rob N. Hood

The Handsomest Man in the World by David Leddick

The Song of a Manchild by Durrell Owens

The Ice Sculptures: A Novel of Hollywood by Michael D. Craig

Between the Palms: A Collection of Gay Travel Erotica by Michael T. Luongo

Aura by Gary Glickman

Love Under Foot: An Erotic Celebration of Feet by Greg Wharton and M. Christian

The Tenth Man by E. William Podojil

Upon a Midnight Clear: Queer Christmas Tales by Greg Herren

Dryland's End by Felice Picano

Whose Eye Is on Which Sparrow? by Robert Taylor

The Handsomest Man
in the World

David Leddick

Southern Tier Editions
Harrington Park Press®
An Imprint of The Haworth Press, Inc.
New York • London • Oxford

Published by

Southern Tier Editions, Harrington Park Press®, an imprint of The Haworth Press, Inc., 10 Alice Street, Binghamton, NY 13904-1580.

PUBLISHER'S NOTE
This is a work of fiction. Names, characters, places, and incidents either are the products of the author's imagination or are used fictitiously, and any resemblance to actual persons, living or dead, business establishments, events, or locales is entirely coincidental.

Cover design by Brooke R. Stiles.
Cover photo (background) by Corbis.
Author's photo by David Vance.

Library of Congress Cataloging-in-Publication Data

Leddick, David.
    The handsomest man in the world / David Leddick.
        p. cm.
        ISBN 1-56023-458-X (soft : alk. paper)
        1. Atomic bomb—Testing—Fiction. 2. Bikini Atoll (Marshall Islands)—Fiction. 3. Gay men—Fiction. 4. Sailors—Fiction. I. Title.
    PS3562.E28444H36 2004
    813'.54—dc21
                                                                            2003012308

For
T. O.

CONTENTS

BIKINI

WAITING

People who do not do anything but be in love, might be more serious and more holy than those who sacrifice their love and their hearts to an idea.

Vincent van Gogh in a letter to his sister

BIKINI

Bikini Bound

We met at Bikini. Everyone always laughs when I tell them that. Most people don't know that Bikini isn't just a bathing suit. It's a place. An atoll actually. In the South Pacific. I met him there, this man I came to love so much, during the hydrogen bomb test. I wonder if anyone else can claim that? There was a sailor on our ship who would sit in a chair on a table in the mess hall and give himself a blow job for a paying audience. So I suppose there must have been *some* sex at Bikini during the tests. But a full-fledged romance? I doubt it.

In fact, we must have met before Bikini, because we were on the same ship out of San Francisco and it must have taken us close to two weeks to get out there. I remember going out on deck one morning and realizing that we were in the South Pacific. The clouds were higher and stringier and the sun was brighter on the ocean and flying fish were darting and winging above the waves to starboard. I had heard of them, but it seemed almost miraculous that they actually existed and *could* fly. Not just darting out of the water and nipping right back in again. They soared. Why, I don't know. To escape larger fish trying to gobble them down? Some mornings we would go on the forecastle and flying fish had actually flown aboard. We must have intercepted their flight, like a large scoop in the sky, or like a large sailing fish. Glumpf . . .they were caught on the bow of our ship and remained there to die.

Fred was aboard, though I don't remember him until we got to Bikini. I was the communications officer and he was one of the radio shack crew. So I must have seen him several times a day, but I have no memory of it. I remember my assistant, a fat lieutenant junior grade, that is. I'm sure he went on to become an optometrist or something like that. Someone in a white coat with an officious air who isn't anything as important as a doctor or a dentist. Shall we call him Lester?

Lester was useless. He had all the emotional equipment of a whiny eighth grader. But isn't that true of a lot of men?

My first conscious memory of Fred must have been that he was large and blond and nice. He had tight, curly blond hair that I remember clearly. And his arms were built up. He had come to the ship after being stationed on Guam, where there was *really* nothing to do. So he and his buddies had gotten into weight lifting. He was big. His arms and chest were very filled out. But he wasn't really muscular. More Rubenesque, if I can use that word. He had beautiful white skin and his body was large and curvy and solid. True flesh. He had true flesh, my Fred.

But I didn't think of him in any romantic way. You know how it is when you're homosexual in the navy. Perhaps you don't. But you kind of keep yourself going with crushes. You have crushes on this man. And this one. You masturbate thinking of them. But you wouldn't really do anything. For one thing, there's nowhere to do it. For a second thing, you're not sure they'd like to do it with you. And for a third thing, there would be hell to pay if you got caught. But I don't remember the third reason ever figuring very importantly. Romantic me—if love came along I was ready to go.

This is probably something you should know about me. Very romantic. *Very* romantic. Standing up in some broom closet with my pants dropped and some guy's cock between my legs would not have been my number. I had gotten all that kind of stuff out of my system before I left grade school.

I was always very adventurous sexually. Lately I've wondered, if perhaps I've returned from a previous existence. Was I some lady of the court who got dropped off in Illinois by mistake? Or perhaps not by mistake. Maybe that's God's little joke. You go through one life as some hard-nosed dame giving men a really bad time. Not putting out. Manipulating the hell out of them. So when you come back you're punished by being put in a man's body, just to sober you up a little bit. It has been sobering, I have to admit.

So by the time I left high school, I had put in a fair amount of time with the same sex. I had my first boyfriend when I was four. He was five. Maybe six. He was always going to marry me when we grew up.

The rat. Where is he now? But that was strictly sex. He was a horny little second grader and remained horny all those years I knew him. He was a very good screw, I'll give him that. But there was never anything romantic about it at all.

I had an enormous crush on another boy in high school who used to hold me and kiss me. Actually I got quite a kick out of that. I think if we had had intercourse I probably would have lost my mind.

There was sort of more of the same through college. But Fred was honestly my first real major start-to-finish romance, and I didn't even recognize it when I first knew him.

I had my eye on others. We were a military detachment aboard a supply ship that had civilian officers. The civilian second mate and the third mate were both tallish, dark, slender, and good-looking. I ricocheted back and forth trying to decide which one I fancied most. The second mate, who was older, was separated from his wife. Seemed a bit depressed most of the time. I didn't have to stand watches and had a lot of free time, so I used to hang around the deck and talk with him during the day. I wasn't really distracting him. There wasn't much to running a ship crossing the Pacific. It was just water out there, lots and lots of wavy, twinkly water that the ship crossed on a southwesterly course day after day after day. The second mate seemed to find me interesting. I suppose I was. My mother always said that I was very outspoken. So I probably gave him my comments on the ship's crew. First the civilian captain, who never emerged from his cabin and received a large wrapped package from the hold each day in the arms of his Filipino steward. The captain amused himself by believing that we thought it was his laundry. We all knew very well that it was a case of beer. The executive officer was shorter, darker, stockier, peppier. He was a navy commander, but I don't remember him ever having a word to say to the men in his command. Certainly never to me. In retrospect, I wonder if he didn't have a wandering eye for other men himself. There was one night at a very drunken shipboard party . . . but more of that later.

At any rate, I chatted my head off with the second mate, who sometimes took his duty on hot days wearing only shorts. Not bad at all. But he ran a poor second to the third mate, who was really sexy.

That is, his *body* was really sexy. *He* wasn't sexy at all. In fact, he was incredibly boring. But I was young. I couldn't tell the difference in those days.

He was slim but muscly. He did exercises in his cabin and often sat out on the deck outside his cabin door in a folding canvas lounge chair he'd brought along. Wearing a very tiny swimsuit. Black. He had black curly hair. Very blue eyes. Was he good-looking? I think maybe he had a pointy nose and small features, but I thought he was very hot stuff. Even in my infatuation I realized there was something vaguely uninteresting about him when he asked me to talk at length about being in a fraternity in college. I think he had perhaps attended some junior college somewhere. He hadn't been to a proper college and was planning to go when his merchant marine time was done. I sat with him when he was on duty rattling on endlessly about fraternity parties and the hazing week before I was accepted into the fraternity and how my fraternity brothers drank themselves into oblivion. He ate it up. I had true glamour in his eyes because I had gone to a large university and had belonged to a fraternity. I didn't tell him that I had left the fraternity house with a few of the brothers and rented an apartment over a post office because I found it boring. It would have been impossible to communicate to my handsome geek that there was life beyond fraternities and that he was already in it. And there was no sexual tingle going on at all. I think I wandered away from those afternoon chats on the bridge deck with my dashing goon because even a crush couldn't survive the fact that instead of me fitting him into my fantasy, he was fitting me into his fantasy. And his fantasy was so dull.

I must have hung around the radio shack shooting off my big mouth to whoever was on duty. Later Fred said, "You always had so much self-confidence. I was very taken with your self-confidence because I had none at all." Funny, isn't it? I wouldn't have called it self-confidence. It just wasn't a lack of self-confidence. I had spent my school days and military career as a low-profile homosexual and had never been criticized or ignored or scorned for it. So I had no reason not to be self-confident. I think I was probably so boy crazy I didn't even have time to wonder if anyone was going to ostracize me for it. This was in the days when guys weren't wandering around making remarks about "queers." They didn't even know what they were. And they wouldn't have categorized the occasional male they were screwing in that way anyway.

So there was Fred in the radio shack. Me, the officer in command who was really just a giddy kind of college kid, dropping by and laughing and telling jokes and telling him about myself. How was I to know he was falling in love with me?

All About the Bomb

An atoll is only a few feet above sea level, at best. Aboard a ship off-shore from an atoll you feel that you are looming high above the sea. Everything in the South Pacific is flat, flat, flat. Even the tallest of the palm trees does not approach the height of a ship's rail. Beyond the curving new-moon shapes of the islands that form the rim of the extinct volcano that is an atoll, the sea stretches away limitlessly. Flat, flat, flat.

Anchored offshore, the USNS *Henrietta Peabody* was a kind of floating hotel. Around us were anchored many other ships. Cargo ships, destroyers, one aircraft carrier: the *Siboney*. The aircraft carrier was there to provide a landing surface for the helicopters that winkled here and there carrying mad scientists and weather experts and high-ranking naval officers to their various rendezvous.

Aboard the *Peabody,* we had absolutely no idea of what the other ships were there to do. Or what they were doing for that matter. Our little LSD landing ship with its drop-ramp front churned back and forth to the island where the civilian technical crew was preparing the first bomb. We provided accommodations for these civilians. They came aboard, took showers, ate in our mess, disappeared. I had come from a largish aircraft carrier, so it seemed very pleasantly relaxed aboard the *Peabody.* The naval contingent numbered perhaps twenty. We were always in uniform, of course, but surrounded by all the civilians in their T-shirts, blue jeans, shorts, short-sleeved shirts badly in need of a good ironing, and khaki pants, it hardly seemed that we were in the navy at all. As head of the communications division, there was very little for me to do. No one particularly wanted to communicate with us. What was there to communicate with us about?

Until the fleet moved for some reason, we sat. I don't remember it as being particularly boring. I had a nice cabin on the upper rank with a little deck. The sea winds blew through. It had two bunks but I was alone. We must have had to report to meals at specific times, but we ate all together in the large mess hall. The officers didn't have their own mess, as we had aboard the carrier. Here we stood in line with our trays and sat at long tables with whomever we pleased. The enlisted men and the handful of officers hung out together. There wasn't much fraternization with the civilian crew. I was pals with the civilian officers who had deck duty but was very grateful that I didn't have to do it myself. Aboard the carrier I had stood deck duty one watch on, two off, which meant that four of every twelve hours I was on the deck, responsible for the ship. It was like working the night shift at the Ford automobile plant. I seemed to do nothing but eat, sleep, and stand my watches. That could get pretty old in a seventeen-day crossing from San Francisco to Yokosuka, Japan.

There was a very adequate ship's library on the *Peabody* and I caught up on a lot of current authors. Philip Wylie had just published *Generation of Vipers*. I was particularly taken with his quote, "Mom, all bon-bons, tits and razzmatazz." I had never read anyone who put Mom in that category. It seemed very daring. I read a lot of Fitzgerald. A lot of Hemingway. I loved Hemingway, which gives you some idea of how young I was. Particularly the Nick Adams stories. "Up in Michigan" I thought was pretty exciting. About some roustabout who slips it to the hired girl.

Of course there was nothing at all about homosexuality. No one even made any cracks about Gertrude Stein and Alice B. Toklas.

So curious, isn't it? The average person couldn't imagine that hanky-panky between persons of the same sex *could* take place. And particularly between persons of the same sex who were public personalities. If you were Gertrude Stein, how could you be a lesbian? You were famous. It's much the same today. Everyone knows there are homosexuals lurking everywhere, but a famous one has to be caught pants down in a public lavatory before the public cares to consider it. Mention Marlon Brando and Wally Cox or Danny Kaye and Sir Laurence Olivier and the looks you get are incredulous. How could this be? They are/were famous. And besides, they were married. Maybe not Wally Cox. Probably he was married to somebody. Everyone in Hollywood.

Not that I particularly longed to know more about homosexuality. It seemed quite out of the question while I was in the hammerlock of the U.S. Navy. In any case, I was hopelessly romantic. I had no desire to give or get a quick blow job in some smelly spot. I wanted love. I wanted to be endlessly locked in someone's arms. Curiously for someone who had been sleeping with boys for many a year, I was not lost to nasty erotic activity. I just wanted a clean-limbed, fresh-faced boyfriend. And I got one.

We must have been fiddling around for several weeks, anchored off Bikini, when a test date was set. It was to be several days later at dawn. We were all to move ship and anchor some thirty-five miles out in formation and get our black goggles ready so we could observe the blast. We were also equipped with roentgen counters, little glass tubes with a bit of paper inside. If we were contaminated by atomic fallout, the paper would change color. We would too, I imagine, but we were very feckless about this. We knew that we had bombed two sites in Japan to bring an end to World War II and that it had been very messy. But the stomach-curdling pictures of the scarred victims suggested only burn victims. Which I'm sure they were. Mysterious particles falling out of the sky or unseeable rays of some unfathomable kind that would destroy the way our insides worked were really beyond us. The sun shone every day, the sea was blue, the sky wasn't quite as blue as the sea, but the sunsets were lurid and hugely streaked in red and purple and looked as though they stretched all the way to Sydney.

I remember being excited. Sort of excited. We gathered on the deck in the darkness, adjusting our goggles. We knew the atoll was somewhere straight off the deck in front of us. The sky began to grow light behind us. When the air was graying we could hear the countdown from the radio shack in the clear. It was coming in uncoded. A voice was counting down the numbers, "Ten, nine, eight, seven, six, five, four, three, two, one." A thin red line burned straight up through the dark sky ahead like a brilliant zipper being pulled up to reveal a scarlet crease in the backdrop of darkness. Then a kind of giant cauliflower began to unfold. I had seen pictures of the atomic bomb with its column and mushroom cloud at the top. This was nothing at all like that. This giant cream cauliflower sat flatly on the ocean. Through the convoluted crevices fire could be seen. Brilliant, orange crimson fire. The cauliflower grew. Soon it reached from side to side of the ocean ahead of us. *This is big,* I thought. *Very big.* It was many miles from one side of that burning cauliflower to the other. From behind me I heard the clicking in the message center. This wasn't encoded either. It read, "Close all hatches and steam for Eniwetok." Eniwetok was the nearest atoll and it was well over one hundred miles away. I rushed the message to the captain and the officers were sent scurrying around the ship to make sure that all doors and hatches were closed and no fans were operating that could pull air in from the outdoors.

The *Peabody* was packed full of civilians who had come aboard just for the night. They were to return ashore in the evening after the blast. But there was no more ashore there, as it turned out.

We steamed all day and all night. It was hot inside that ship. With all the hatches closed there was no daylight below the main deck and all the electricity was blazing. The grand staircase to the dining area—the *Peabody* carried dependents in the course of its regular duties so it had some of the characteristics of a passenger ship—had a body lying on every tread. There were so many people aboard that every passageway, every public area was jammed with standing, squatting, sitting civilians. The captain asked the officers if they would go among the civilians and if someone seemed to be on the verge of passing out to take him to an officer's cabin and let him lie in a bunk. Our cabins were at the top of the ship. The portholes admitted daylight, and it was the coolest area. The ship's passage created wind that cooled these upper cabins, even if they were exposed to the heat of the sun. The officers trolled about and kept moving passengers in and out of their cabins to recover from the heat below decks. What was going on in the engine room without fans I can't imagine. I certainly didn't check it out.

Through all of this I have no memory of Fred. He must have been present in the radio shack in his unironed blue chambray shirt and navy dungarees; no pleats and flaring at the bottom, a web belt holding them up, solid black shoes. The officers wore solid brown shoes. No messing about with sandals. The civilian officers could wear shorts and sandals. But there were no such things in the naval officers' wardrobes.

I didn't sleep in my cabin that night but kept rotating those who were sick from the heat in and out. In the early hours of the next morning the captain of the fleet radioed that portholes and hatches could be opened. As the dawn came we could see the lights of Eniwetok, immediately at sea level, like floating sampans. Another atoll, barely out of the sea. As we anchored I could see a Jeep running along a narrow ridge of sand that was so close to the water and so devoid of foliage that the little vehicle seemed to be jouncing along on the tops of the waves.

The last time I was really drunk was on Eniwetok. The atoll was primarily a naval base and there was an officers' club and an enlisted men's club ashore. Although all the civilian passengers had to remain aboard, the naval contingent was sent ashore in whaleboats for an evening out. I knew all was not well when I saw an officer leaving the club. He hit both doorjambs, left and right, as he staggered through. And they were about six feet apart. The club was built on a Hawaiian theme with broad verandas, a thatched roof, a wide entryway, and a prominent bar. I guess everyone drank a lot because there was really nothing else to do. We had all explored every nook and cranny of each other's conversations by now, so starting the evening with six martinis seemed like an excellent idea.

A storm was brewing when we gathered again on a pier in the inky night to reembark for the *Peabody*. The whaleboat came alongside and we clambered in, but as we beat away from land the waves became higher. And higher. By the time we reached the ship the waves were nearing ten feet, which meant that when the whaleboat came alongside the *Peabody,* we were rising very high and falling very low beside the rope ladder that hung down from the doors that were flung open on the side of the ship. And we were very drunk.

As the whaleboat rose to the level of the rope ladder, each man had to fling himself against the side of the larger ship. The whale boat immediately dropped far below him. If he fell he'd fall into the boat, breaking bones if he was lucky. Or he'd fall between the whaleboat and the ship and hope someone would fish him out. It was terrifying, but no one spoke of it. Splat, splat, splat, each of us in turn stood on unsteady feet in the unsteady open boat and hurled ourselves toward the rope ladder, clinging like frightened spiders, then clambering toward the lighted opening where welcoming hands pulled us in.

The next morning as we steamed back toward Bikini, there was no part of my body that was not painful to touch, such was my hangover. To lie in bed was unbearable, to put on clothing hurt, to sit was unthinkable. I'm sure I sulked around the radio shack, stood about on the bridge, wandered the decks feeling sorry for myself as we zipped back over the glossy blue waves under the blazing sun. Whether Fred had gone ashore with the other enlisted men I cannot say. He must have. No one stays aboard a ship when he doesn't have to. And Fred wasn't averse to a drink or two. Later, when we knew each other better, he would say, "Everyone should get really drunk once a week. Just to relax." I wonder if he still does. I think not.

Back at Bikini

As we entered the lagoon, we passed the little island where the civilians had been quartered. There was nothing left on it. The bomb had been detonated on a platform in the middle of the lagoon. There was talk that the explosion had been six times larger than anticipated. If the flat, treeless island we passed was any indication, it was at least that.

We anchored, and by the next day word came in that rain clouds had carried contamination from the bomb far north. The clouds had rained on a Japanese fishing vessel. Trouble was brewing.

We were kept from the worst of the news, only reading about it later when we returned from the tests. But it was clear something was awry. There was a great coming and going of weather experts. The navy weather staff was replaced with one from the air force. But what must have been furor in Washington translated into long, hot, boring days aboard the *Henrietta Peabody*.

It was a bit Kafkaesque. There was to be a series of six tests in all. One down, five to go. Very rapidly it was announced that a second test was to be performed in two days. In the early morning hours we steamed out to sea, anchored, came on deck in our black glasses, and as we approached countdown I heard a message clicking in. I dashed to the radio shack, quickly decoded it, and found that the test was canceled and would be rescheduled. *That* became our routine. Scheduled tests, up early to watch, and then cancellation. It certainly was a way to give people something to do every day.

This went on for a long time before there was a second test. We had originally been scheduled to be at Bikini for six tests. We had now been there for the six weeks and the *second* test hadn't taken place yet, let alone the four others scheduled to take place.

The ship settled into a somnolent routine. Most of the civilians had found accommodations on other ships in the fleet. A few were left

with us. But no one went back ashore. Every day we swung on our anchor in the sun that rose without fail, blazed all day, and sank away in
great streams of tropical color.

There were no real duties, except vague preparations for tests that
did not happen. The highlight of the day was the evening motion picture. Unfortunately, movies had been provided only for the six weeks
anticipated, so we began to repeat movies. We were at Bikini for four
months all together, so repeating the films only satisfied the ship's
crew to a modest degree. *Gentlemen Prefer Blondes* was the only film
shown *every* evening, and finally only certain hard-core viewers still
watched Marilyn Monroe and Jane Russell strut their stuff night after
night. As is the case with many homosexuals, I enjoyed watching
pretty women and was often among those nightly viewers. I don't
think I ever wanted to trade places with Marilyn or Jane, nor did I
want men's eyes to follow me as I wandered about. Although they
did. I was frequently admired for my nice ass by straight men, but I
never paid much attention. I couldn't see it and never took these at-
tentions very seriously.

I had a roommate in college who watched me walk across the room
one day and mumbled that he wished I had a sister. He was the one
that lay down on top of me on my bed as I was studying. I had been
lying face down. He was pressed into my buttocks and wanted to play
Mom and Dad. He didn't fit my idea of a romantic hero, I guess. I
often think that if he had, we would probably have taken a room together outside the dorm, and I would have been getting mine regularly right up to the time that he went into dentistry college. I might
be married to him today. On these little decisions do our lives turn. If
you're not desperate, you finally wind up having a lot less sex. Is that
good or bad? I never can decide.

Later, when I was in a fraternity, I had been assigned to dig up
flower beds along the sidewalk. Bending over to pull weeds in shorts
attracted a car full of yahoos who shouted, whistled, and were profoundly disappointed when it was me who stood up. The nice ass
turned out to be attached to a boy. A very period scenario.

Aboard the aircraft carrier I had had a married roommate who liked
to put his hands on my ass as I went up a ladder (staircase to you civil-

ians) ahead of him. He was kind of sexy, but I was still young enough to think that a married man wouldn't be interested in any hanky-panky. I wouldn't have been too keen on adultery, anyway. Never was. Still am not.

So yes, there I was aboard the *Henrietta Peabody* with my nice ass. But nobody seemed to care, as far as I could tell anyway. I was con-ducting my simple-minded little flirtations with civilian deck officers. Every week I changed my masturbation fantasies to some new guy, just to keep up some enthusiasm.

Strangely enough, when I look back, I remember that my Fred, Fred Jorgensen, had been one of my masturbation fantasies for a short period. Replaced with whom, I wonder? I guess his blondness and his muscles must have caught my attention for awhile. But he really was never in it with the dark-haired, blue-eyed, streamlined civilian offi-cer I fancied so much. I've always fancied those taut, fine-muscled, slim bodies. Rather like racehorses. There's something about them that suggests they could deliver a really great fuck.

I really didn't care all that much, to be honest with you. I was prob-ably more interested in the ship's library than in any of the men aboard. I was working my way through it. The only other person who ever read its books was our ship's doctor, who had been called back into the navy from civilian life. He told me one day while we were in the library together that he had had a vasectomy. I was very im-pressed, even though I had to ask him to tell me what that was. Stopping your sperm. Well, not exactly. But stopping your potency. It made the backs of my legs quiver just thinking about it. Fiddling around with all those delicate little tubes and membranes.

I was happy enough. I had my books and sex fantasies. I've often thought how different it was for me and, say, the officer with the va-sectomy. He was there in the real world. Longing to get back to his wife. Longing to get back to the civilian world and his medical prac-tice.

I had never been in the civilian world as he knew it. I had spent my life to that point in school. And I had always had an interior world filled with imagining what it was like to sleep with this guy or that guy. I actually slept with a fair number of them to keep me in contact with reality from time to time.

And here I was aboard ship with a lot of guys. My fantasies could plug right along. Plenty of material to think about and masturbate over. Maybe even uncover a lover. I was leading a rich and exciting, albeit hidden, life.

The heterosexuals were cut off from their sex lives. There were no women around for them to fantasize over. They were left with looking at Marilyn Monroe and Jane Russell. No rich fantasy life was available to them aboard the *Henrietta Peabody*. There was just frustration and boredom.

So it goes on in the civilian world today. Heterosexual men can fantasize about the women they see, but they know there are endless complications once they dip that wick somewhere outside their homes.

Homosexuals move in a world where the straightest-looking, straightest-acting guys can suddenly try to slap the make on you. And if they do, chances are slight . . . shall we say none . . . that there will be complications unless you really want them. One of my straight friends had a conversation with me about this not long ago. I said, "At least in homosexual relationships when the romance, the sex, the excitement is over and there is nothing left, men tend to not stay together. But with heterosexual relationships things drag on forever, with the children, the real estate, the mortgages replacing love as a focus of interest."

My heterosexual friend said, "The homosexual lifestyle has a lot to recommend it. It's only the sex part I boggle at."

Hit the Beach

I want you to understand something. There was nothing to do at Bikini. Nothing. N-O-T-H-I-N-G. We were on a ship anchored in sunny waters. Shall we say hot. Aside from the occasional flurries of activity at dawn over projected bomb detonations that never occurred, there were no shipboard duties. The *Henrietta Peabody* wasn't a warship, so the enlisted men did not have to keep the ship in a constant state of readiness. We were not steaming anywhere, so there was nothing to do during the watches. Even for the head of the communication division, damn little communication was going on.

The captain decided that the enlisted men should be allowed to go ashore for a little swimming and a beer bust. What did we know about contamination? No one seemed to think this was a problem. Several of the junior officers were selected to go ashore with them to supervise the festivities. It promised to be dreary. We couldn't get drunk with them. We couldn't get drunk at all, actually. And I certainly wasn't going to hang around with my porcine little assistant, Lester, who had been designated as the other junior officer to go ashore.

An LSD came alongside for us. Could I have been wearing a tie and overseas cap? Perhaps I was allowed to go in bathing trunks and a T-shirt. The enlisted men were in their blue jeans and white caps. They were already comfortable. Many cases of beer were dropped aboard. And several big garbage cans of ice.

We forged directly across the lagoon, and the LSD dropped its big front-end, landing right on the shore. The island was a not very large crescent of sand backed by palm trees and underbrush. Before we left the executive officer said, "Just don't go in the underbrush. If you stay out on the sand you'll be okay." Nothing about not going in the water. If the sailors hadn't been allowed to go in the water, there would have been little reason to let them go ashore. That must have been the thinking. What little thinking there was.

Immediately upon hitting the sand, the sailors tore off their uniforms to reveal a fascinating variety of bathing outfits. Some had no trunks, so kept on their baggy white underpants with the three-button fronts and the little adjusting ties on the hips. We all had the same underwear in the navy, officers and enlisted men alike. White T-shirts and those big-bottomed white cotton underpants. We had all been brought up wearing jockey undershorts, so clambering into those billowing bloomers was like wearing our grandfather's underpants. I don't remember anyone complaining.

It was already bizarre enough wearing exactly the same clothing every day. I wonder how often the sailors changed their clothing. Officers were required to be very spic and span, so we had a fresh khaki shirt and pants every single day, direct from the ship's laundry. Aboard the aircraft carrier we had stewards whose responsibility it was to drag our laundry back and forth, make our beds, clean our cabins, and wait on us in the officer's mess. They were black or Filipino, always. My own personal steward stole my wristwatch and money from my cabin the day he was discharged. I was really glad he did. I hated being waited on. And I hated that the stewards were all black and Filipino. There were other black enlisted men in the communication division and elsewhere aboard ship, but not many. I guess when you're homosexual the standard is not based upon race, creed, or place of national origin. It's beauty. It's impossible to think of a black man as being lesser. He's humpy or he's not humpy. Sex, the great equalizer.

Did I ever tell you how I drove Ensign Posey mad aboard the aircraft carrier? It's not really relevant to my story about Bikini except to demonstrate for you I *can* be devious.

Ensign Posey was in a cabin directly across the passage from me on the carrier. We were in a warren of little cabins below the water line where the junior officers were stabled. I never had trouble sleeping there even though my worst fear is being trapped in a sinking ship.

Ensign Posey was from Chicago or Oak Park or Lake Forest or one of those places. It's so hard to imagine that people from Chicago could be snobbish about where they live, but I guess they are. Ensign Posey had a girlfriend or a fiancée who sent him packages of food. Ensign Posey did not open these packages. He placed the food on a shelf in his cabin and there it sat. Ensign Posey was not a sharer. He did not share, the worst possible crime in the world of kindergarten. And aboard a U.S. naval ship.

I took matters into my own hands. While Ensign Posey was on duty on the bridge, I entered his cabin and with a razor blade slit open the bottom of his boxes of Ritz crackers, his Fannie Farmer chocolates, his chocolate chip cookies, his potato chips, his Triscuits, and his Pecan Sandies. Please don't think I gorged. I ate a little here. A little bit there. Light grazing. I never ate *everything* that was in the package. I have some standards. And then I sealed things up neatly with Scotch tape and put them back on the shelf. I put a little bit of wastepaper in to keep the weight unsuspicious. I figured he was never going to eat those things anyway. They were just going to dry up and dessicate there. And I was always hungry. I hate waste. Hate it. There really wasn't any alternative.

Except that I didn't realize that Ensign Posey was batty. After he went around the bend, my pal John David Spangler told me, "I should have sensed something. We were on the bridge together and I asked him where he went to school and he said, 'First I went to kindergarten at Grove Street Elementary and then in first grade we moved and I went to Judson Corners Grade School' and so on all through college. I had a feeling then that things were not all right." Things got very not all right one evening when we were approaching Japan. Ensign Posey went to the executive officer's cabin and told him that someone was hiding in his clothes locker and was looking at him through the little hole by the handle. It was true that there were small round holes just above the handles on the metal locker doors. I had noticed them myself but never thought about looking through one. The executive officer asked, "How big is this hole?" I guess he thought he shouldn't be too quick to jump to conclusions that it was unlikely there was a stowaway in Ensign Posey's locker. Then Ensign Posey cinched it. He said, "I know someone's in there because he comes out when I'm not there and eats the food that I have stored on the shelf in my cabin. I opened it and it's all full of newspaper and stuff like that. He's been opening the boxes and sealing them up again."

This was too much for the executive officer, who had the medical orderlies come and take Ensign Posey away to sick bay, where he stayed until we tied up in Yokosuka, and then he was whisked away to a mental hospital.

I was incensed when I heard this story. I had *not* eaten everything. That Ensign Posey. He not only didn't share, he didn't tell the whole truth.

I ran into Ensign Posey and a keeper in San Francisco one evening when I was out beating around the usual haunts of the Purple Onion, the Fat Black Pussy Cat, Goman's Gay Nineties, the House of Blue Lights, and the Tonga Room at the Fairmont Hotel. Ensign Posey looked like he had experienced a fair amount of electroshock. His keeper was kind of good-looking and regarded me suspiciously. I wondered if he was making love to Ensign Posey as part of his return to reality. I felt guilty, but not too guilty. Maybe Ensign Posey would have slipped through the navy and finished his duty with no one finding out he was completely bonkers. And certainly doing some time in a navy loony bin can't do anyone a world of good. But chances are his destiny would have unfolded whether I ate his food or not. I like to think that at least all that food did not go to waste. Waste not want not, you know. At least that's what I tell myself. To my credit, I confided in no one aboard ship that I had eaten his food. Not my roommate, Kenneth. Nor my best friend, John David Spangler. No one. Not until now.

But to return to the beach. My piggy little assistant Lester sat right down by the garbage can, which had many beers pushed down in the ice it contained. The enlisted men first rushed into the water and flailed about. I don't think many of them could swim. There was a lot of splashing and dunking of one another. Lester didn't go in. He kept his shirt on. I don't think he wanted us to see his pudgy body. I didn't go in because I couldn't figure out a way to go in and swim without looking like I was being careful not to join the sailors. They always had one eye out to see which officers were highfalutin' and I didn't want to be put in that category.

I said to Lester, "You stay here." I decided to cross the island and have a swim on the other side. Since the island was about 100 yards wide it wasn't going to be hard to do.

I remembered the executive officer's warning and tried not to come into too much physical contact with clacking palm fronds and the scruffy shrubs underfoot. I pushed my way through very quickly, and on the other side a reversed crescent of white sand led down to the baby-blue water. The water was almost exactly the same temperature as the air, so I had to look down to see if my legs were in the water. They were. The bottom is very shallow around the atoll islands, so I had to struggle quite a way out. I took off my trunks and strung them over one shoulder so I wouldn't lose them and struck out with a slow crawl parallel to the beach.

I have only two physical skills. I can swim well and I'm a good shot. You don't expect effete types like myself to be able to do anything well that requires some kind of physical capability. Certainly no one in my family ever encouraged me to try. My father and brothers threw up their hands long ago about my lack of interest, not to mention skill, in golf and tennis. I should mention riding, too, I suppose. I was forced to ride, but I always hated horses. I could never ignore what it would be like to have one fall on me. One fell on Cole Porter, you know. Then rolled over and fell on him again. Crushed both legs. A homosexual with two crushed legs is not a pretty sight. Not that Cole was an extravagantly pretty sight to begin with.

So when I was twenty-one I refused to mount a horse ever again. And have stuck by my resolve. I swim. I astonished the other officers with my marksmanship. I guess I do both these things well because I like to. I really enjoy plunging in water and zooming about. All part of my liking to get to the bottom of things, I guess. And I enjoy shooting because of the precision. You see the thing flying about—only clay disks, I'm not about to shoot any animals—and you lead with the nose of your gun and pow, it's gone. At dinner from time to time some hearty type asks me if I hunt and I always tell him, "I could never kill an animal." Then I add, "But there are some human beings I could shoot." I mean it. I've known some really horrible people. No one could regret a sniper picking them off from some nearby clock tower.

Aboard the aircraft carrier the officers had small arms drill. Tin cans were thrown in the air from the fantail and we shot them. It wasn't easy with the ship lifting and falling. But even there I had a pretty high success rate, the cans flying ever higher and falling into the churning wake behind the ship. The other officers were impressed. But not overly. They just thought it was sort of a fluky thing I could do. As though I were double jointed, or something like that.

The water felt great over my naked body and after I swam back and forth a couple of times I floated about and thought how nice it would be to have one of my imaginary loves with me, and I fooled around with myself and had an orgasm. It was too beautiful there in the water with the sand and the sun and blowing palms not to. I'm sure I was the only one who did this during our beach outing that day. That's probably why the executive officer said the underbrush was out of bounds. He was probably afraid the drunken horde would drag one another out of sight and have their way.

When I slipped back through the underbrush, the sailors were well advanced in their drunkenness and were in the wrestling stage. There was a lot of crotch pressing amid the struggling, so they were getting a certain amount of sexual tension out of the way. Or maybe making it worse. Some of the men could no longer stand, so Lester and I dragged them into the shade where they wouldn't be burned to a cinder. They seemed quite contented to lie there with a bit of drool slipping from their lips.

I'm sure Fred wasn't there that day or I would have noticed. He had a big, beautiful body and there was no one there with a big, beautiful body. As Lester and I hauled the bodies up and laid them in a row, I particularly noticed how unappealing they were. Most men's bodies are not very appealing. But I suppose you've noticed that.

The beer was almost gone. The sun was perceptibly slipping toward the horizon. And the LSD was on schedule. It dug its way through the water toward us and dropped its door. We corralled the men who could walk reasonably well and got them to help their staggering pals aboard the boat. We laid them out on the bottom, cleaned up the cans on the beach by throwing them into garbage containers, looked about, and clambered aboard. The door cranked shut.

When we got back to the ship I realized that a good many of the men were not going to be able to climb the rope ladder back to the open door above our heads. The deck officer could clearly see the situation, so he got the duty crew to swing out a crane and lower a cargo net. I thought it was a little dangerous but had no better idea, so we laid the mumbling, groaning bodies out on the flat net and had them haul it away, with arms and legs and heads lolling out of it. As long as they didn't clonk it down on the deck it would be all right. The deck officer watched carefully, and after three lowerings and raisings we got everyone aboard. The enlisted men who could had already climbed the ladder. Lester and I had done the loading. He thought it was a lot of fun. I'll bet he's still talking about it today. I am.

We later had a number of those outings, but I had the good sense to ration the beer to ten cans a man after that. Ten cans would let them get really drunk but not to a point where they couldn't walk or climb ladders. You learn worthwhile things in the navy.

Party Time

Time was dragging its feet at Bikini. We had been out for more than two months now, nearly three. Two more tests had taken place, after many, many false alarms and cancellations. One was a spindly little fire column with a little ball of smoke at the top, almost like a disappointing Fourth of July fireworks. The other was a little clumpy ball of smoke on the horizon. The thrill was definitely gone.

The enlisted men decided to throw a party. Not all the officers were invited. I was, but my second-in-command Lester had not been told about it. He wouldn't be disappointed if he never knew it happened.

It was to be a costume party. I wore shorts and the top to my white dress uniform. Stress those legs. And I'm sure that I wore the hat I had found when we were ashore one day.

We had made several more trips to that little strip of beach, and I crossed the tiny island to swim by myself each time. Returning through that dry and dusty underbrush, I found a hat woven from a palm frond. Sitting waiting for the sailors to get sufficiently drunk to return to the ship, I analyzed the way the hat was made. It was quite simple really. The center strip of the frond made the hatband. The leaves on one side were interwoven to form the crown. The leaves on the lower side then were woven together to make a brim. It looked complicated, but when I pulled a palm frond off a tree and tried to copy the hat, I found it was quite simple. I then became very popular making frond hats for everyone. Once you got the head size correct, the rest was easy.

There were many other palm frond hats at the sailors' party, as well as paper streamers that had been twisted and strung across the ceiling of the cabin. The streamers were made of toilet paper. Where could this party have been? The enlisted men were probably housed six to a cabin and it must have been in one of these. I don't remember. I do remember that there were not a whole lot of sailors present. Perhaps twelve to fifteen in all aboard the *Peabody*. They didn't have to sleep all packed together as enlisted men had aboard the aircraft carrier. There bunks were hung six deep from floor to ceiling in one large compartment that held more than 100 men. Each man had about two feet between his bunk and the one above him. I would have hated sleeping in one of the lower ones with all those bodies above me ready to collapse downward. I used to inspect the ship on the night watches and go through those huge spaces lit with blue light, the bodies packed in every direction. Everyone sleeping away with no problem. The sleep itself hung in the air. I had to fight my way through and try not to slump to the deck myself, snoring with my flashlight still clutched in my hot hand.

In the party cabin on the *Henrietta Peabody* the light was bluish, too. Probably from smoke. It was dim. In the center of the floor was a large garbage can filled with ice and beer. The drink du jour. To my surprise, the only other officer was the executive officer, the second in command to the captain. Dark, squat, full-bodied but not bad-bodied, I noticed. He was wearing only a pair of khaki shorts and his cap and was already quite drunk when I arrived.

Music was playing and some men were dancing. This was in no way a gay party. The word "gay" wasn't even used then. This was a more traditional sailors' party, where everyone amused himself as best he could, very much like the crossing-the-equator parties that required the crew to get into wigs made of mops and brassieres collected from God knows where. And run around humping the captain's lap. The Romans, the Celts, and the cavemen before them must have had similar parties. It actually must have been quite jolly and nice before everyone got all caught up in dividing people into categories of who was homosexual and who was not. I think men can have a lot of fun running around acting silly without actually kissing and putting their penises inside one another's orifices.

At least at this party they did. It was hot in the stifling little room and the music was loud. What could they have been playing? Probably Elvis Presley. No shirts. Some had on cutoff jeans. There was a fair amount of flesh on display. But short flesh. No one was very tall ex-

cept Fred. He was there but wearing a T-shirt and jeans. I noticed he
had great arms. I am a sucker for arms.

One of the cheeky little redheaded guys from the deck crew asked
me to dance with him and I obliged. I'm a good dancer and we had
fun. But it was decorous. No crotch jamming or anything like that.
After all, I was an officer, which equates in the average sailor's mind to
being something like a lady. You aren't going to grab an officer's tits.

Everyone had to take a turn dancing with me, once they saw that I
could dance and was a good sport. I looked down on the tops of blond
crewcuts, long sleek-black dark hair, curly brown hair. I put my
hands on their sweat-wet shoulders, they clutched my wet hand, and
we cut rugs, did slow numbers, laughed, and chatted. There wasn't
anything even faintly romantic about any of it. At one point I stood in
the garbage can filled with water and ice and beer just to cool off. I
danced with Fred once, which was a relief because he was my height.
He wasn't an energetic dancer, but I could put my arm on his shoulders and I felt his large hand on my back through my damp uniform
top. I didn't take my jacket off. An officer has to maintain some standards. Our executive officer didn't dance with anyone, I noticed, but
stumbled around the edges of the room tossing down beers steadily.

I tell you all this because this was no literary romantic scenario,
Fred and I. I did not think of him as a sexual prospect, either. I wanted
the men to have fun. They were, after all, *my* men. At least the ones
that were in the communication division. If they thought it was amusing to have their officer cavorting with them, I was all for it. But if
anyone had any other ideas in mind, they were carefully concealed.
There was a lot of belly to belly going on and grabbing and hugging,
but all wreathed in beerish vapors so no one could be accused the next
day of acting "queer."

When some men started throwing up I excused myself. I knew
anyone who threw up on me would be very unhappy the next day and
since I wasn't drunk and had had very little beer, I was ready to go to
bed. I was something like a navy canteen hostess. I had danced. I had
laughed. They had had fun with me. My work was done.

I went up to my cabin on the upper deck. The executive officer was
standing in front of my door when I got there. Actually leaning against

the railing across from my door. Short and tanned very dark, kind of a belly, there was certainly something sexy about him. But the idea of a senior officer being interested in sleeping with me didn't cross my mind. I was such a simp. I was so sure that the navy was just as simple and clear-cut as its regulations. I had every intention of having a male lover and very romantic sex life eventually. But after I got out of the navy.

The executive officer growled from under the bill of his cap, "Hi." He had a can of beer in each hand.

"Hi," I said.

"Want a beer?" he said, holding one out.

"No, I've had plenty," I said, opening my cabin door.

"Want to talk?" he said.

"Come in," I said. "But I'm really tired. I'm going to go to sleep very soon."

He dropped his body into the lower bunk. This was very unusual. Senior officers never fraternized with junior officers. Never came to their cabins. And he was a commander. Commander Frattilillo. Could that have been his name? He was Italian. I remember that. He took his hat off and put his arm across his eyes.

"I sure miss my wife," he mumbled.

I got the picture. He was lonely. I was going to have to cheer him up a little. I have a strong maternal instinct. Clara Barton would have loved me. Walt Whitman was a nurse during the Civil War and loved his charges. Abraham Lincoln passing by in his carriage as Whitman walked down the street said, "Well, he looks like a man." So rumors must have been rife about Walt even then. Not that he cared.

"We'll be leaving here soon, I'm sure," I said, sitting down on the metal chair by my desk.

"Not soon enough," he said. He looked at me. His eyes were really sad. And really drunk. In addition to the fact that he was a senior officer, it would never have occurred to me to be interested in someone markedly older than myself either. Poor Commander Frattilillo. He could have hugged me and kissed me. He could have lowered his shorts and bobbled about between my legs and I wouldn't have really minded. It just didn't occur to me that this was where it was all heading. And perhaps I'm wrong. Perhaps it wasn't.

"Think I'll just sleep," he said, and put his beers down on the floor and closed his eyes.

"If you want to," I said, thinking this was mucho bizarre behavior but that it wasn't my decision. He was senior to me. The decisions were up to him.

I put on a clean T-shirt and clean undershorts. I switched off the lights and was careful, when I put my foot on the edge of the lower bunk to clamber into the top, that I didn't step on the commander. I usually slept in the lower bunk, but I wasn't really inconvenienced. In the morning the commander was gone. The bunk was messed up, but he was gone with his beers. One of the first things one of the men said to me when I came into the radio shack after breakfast was, "I saw the commander wandering around on the deck last night. He was half dressed and really drunk."

"Was this after the party ended below decks?" I said.

"It was late. Real late. Four or so. Man, do I have a headache. But I bet the commander's got a real one. He was plastered. He stumbled right into me."

The poor commander. He had really wanted to get laid. He just wanted to put that little barrel body of his up against someone. Anyone. And probably thought blond-and-swishy me was a good bet. Poor guy. He was right but a little too early.

In Hawaii

Look, there's a lesson for all of us in here somewhere. Because love just came dropping out of nowhere when I least expected it. So fast that it could have slipped right through my fingers, I was so unprepared. Just like when someone shoots a basketball at you when you're not ready. Do you remember that game? Someone in the center has the ball and everyone else is in a circle, and if he suddenly shoots the ball at you and you drop it, you have to get in the center. I guess falling in love is like when you're in the center of the circle. You're "it" and it's uncomfortable. You can understand why lots of people don't want to be in love. You're not an onlooker anymore.

We had finally wound things up at Bikini. I really don't remember the rest of the tests. They were certainly little dribbles and drabbles. One was underwater, I think, so there wasn't much to see. So more than two months later than we had planned to return to the States, we lifted anchor and set sail.

Nothing was different during that voyage to Hawaii. We were stopping in Honolulu to pick up military families as passengers. The high command probably thought they should try to do something useful with us after all that futzing around at Bikini. So we plunked along, out of the South Pacific, into the mid-Pacific. The days a little cooler. The sunsets a little less spectacular. There were no more beer busts. Everyone was more than ready to return. I was still the closeted lieutenant, j.g., really not at all unhappy with my lot. I probably had been brutalized by the service and had reduced my sexual expectations to zero, but it didn't bug me. Truly.

In Honolulu I made plans to meet Fred ashore. Yes, we had become much more friendly. I always love to shoot off my big mouth and I'm sure I sat around the radio shack and explained the world and how it worked to anyone who would listen. It was most often his large, blond presence that was trapped there. That appealed to me.

At any rate, we made plans to meet. Probably someplace like the bar at the Royal Hawaiian. The outdoor one that revolved. Where they occasionally tied a rope to some very drunken person's leg and a nearby tree, so as the bar turned he was snatched off his stool and left lying flat on his back in the sand, much to the amusement of the other patrons who passed by above.

However our meeting was planned, it didn't happen. I had arranged to have lunch with the only person from my hometown who lived in Honolulu, a classmate of one of my older brothers, who had been a neighbor during my childhood. I had always been impressed by her wittiness and sophistication. Oh, yes, even in Illinois there were a few witty people. Muriel McGuire, now Muriel Somebody-or-other.

Muriel and I met in the court of some restaurant. We ate salads with a lot of pineapple, drank exotic drinks with fruit and gin and fizzy water. We laughed a lot. It was really fun to be an amusing grown-up with amusing Muriel in exotic Hawaii. It was the first *real* fun I'd had since we left San Francisco, and we still had six days steaming ahead of us to get there from Honolulu. We were leaving at six o'clock that evening.

I'm sure that I went to the rendezvous where I was to meet Fred. I remember that we both wore civilian clothes so that there would be no comment about officers fraternizing with enlisted men. When I had been aboard the aircraft carrier, the executive officer saw me laughing with our weather forecaster on the flight deck. The forecaster was a college graduate, a big reader, and fun to talk to. About my age but I never found him attractive, although he was.

Being friendly with enlisted men was taboo, so the executive officer called me to his cabin. A little fat man who looked very out of place in a naval uniform. His nervous little eyes always made me uneasy. Like a tethered snake who could strike you at any moment if you weren't very careful. He said, "You must remember that familiarity breeds contempt." I couldn't believe I was actually hearing someone say those words. "Only if you're contemptible," I said and stepped backward out of his cabin door standing very straight. I was really angry that someone short and not good-looking would have the temerity to criticize me. I thought that being tall, blond, and American put me in a class above his kind of criticism. I think he thought so, too, because I never heard any repercussions for being such a snotty brat with him. He probably expected someone like me to be snotty and let it go at that. I was lucky.

But I never found Fred in the hordes of naval personnel streaming through the bar where we were to meet. And time was running out. I had to be back aboard the ship and in uniform to help board the passengers well before we sailed.

I took a taxi back, changed into my uniform, and went down to the mess to have something to eat before reporting to the radio shack. The good-looking civilian officer—the one who had been married, not the humpy, well-muscled one—was sitting directly opposite me when I sat down. There were others at the long table. He looked at me. I realized that he was very drunk. He said, "Don't you realize that I'm in love with you?" I was completely thrown. We were within earshot of some of the other officers, though they were not paying any attention to us. I couldn't imagine how to respond. So I stood up, pushed my chair out of the way, and walked rapidly out of the mess. I was stunned and on automatic. I couldn't even think clearly about what he had said. Except I knew it was a conversation that I didn't know how to enter into. And that it was very dangerous.

Without thinking where I was going, I automatically went to the radio shack to take shelter. Just to be somewhere familiar. As I entered, Fred was sitting at the transmitter. Back in uniform, too. The familiar blue chambray shirt and jeans. He turned as I came in and looked up at me, a stricken expression on his face. "Where were you?" he said. "I looked everywhere for you this afternoon and never found you. Don't you know I love you?" Pow. It was like taking a one-two punch. My brain stopped. But somehow deep inside of me somewhere I knew I couldn't throw this away as I just had the encounter in the mess hall below decks. I started crying.

There was a small balcony-style deck beside the radio shack and the door was open. I went out there. Fred came out and stood beside me. We had left port and were steaming past Diamond Head. It was the end of the day and golden light was pouring over that famous snub-nosed point of land. The sea was navy blue with frisky little white-

caps. We were heading off into the coming darkness. It was such a romantic cliché. Even then I was aware of it. "What's happening?" I
kept asking myself. Here I was right in the middle of a very romantic
movie scenario without a moment's preparation. I don't think I said
much. Fred was telling me how frightened he had become that something might have happened to me, how he had never felt this way
about anyone before in his whole life.

I think you get the picture. I couldn't really say I felt the same way
because I didn't. On the other hand, I wasn't going to say that it was
out of the question because that wasn't true either. My assistant, fat
Lester, suddenly appeared in the doorway. "Hey, what are you guys
doing out there?" he said in an alarmed voice. He knew something
wasn't right but not exactly what. I turned like an unleashed python
and hissed, "Get out of here!" I must have had plenty of venom, because he jumped backward. I wondered if he would tell people he had
seen Fred and me holding hands on the little platform by the radio
shack and crying, but I thought, "Who the hell does he know?"

Fred and I did not go directly down to my cabin and get it on. Poor
guy. I don't think he realized that when you fall in love with another
man you're supposed to sock it to him. I don't think I realized it myself. Maybe you're not. I know it passed through my mind that maybe
we should try it, and I think if he had really wanted to put the blocks
to me then and there it would have happened. Chances are we would
have gotten away with it. I had been assigned a larger cabin to myself
away from the other officers. Probably someone who outranked me
got my former cabin on the top deck.

Fred and I did sit in my cabin and talk a lot during those days en
route to San Francisco. Having him in my cabin with the door closed
was already very daring. If it had been a real military vessel it would
have been completely out of the question. But there were so many civilians and wives and children milling about, no one was paying too
much attention to where the personnel were and what they were doing.

What could we possibly have talked about? I was sexually excited
by Fred. I wanted that big body to be crawling all over me. But it
wasn't one of those "I must have you in me" situations where you drag

the guy down on the floor and tear his clothes off. Although we got to that later.

Maybe I misremember the drama. Maybe I underestimate what I felt. But I think my drive was toward getting laid. Not toward having a great romance. When we arrived in San Francisco, all the military personnel reported immediately to naval headquarters for new assignments. There were no immediate assignments for anyone except Lester. He was sent off to the East Coast posthaste. Which left me as the only officer with some six communications personnel. They had all stayed at a rooming house on Sacramento Street while waiting to join the *Henrietta Peabody* and decided to return there. I'm sure my intentions were not to let Fred slip from my grasp. I'm not sure I planned that we would take a room together. There were two levels of activity going on at the same time here. One was the young happy-go-lucky officer who decides to stay with the enlisted men while awaiting orders. He shares a room with one of the men to save on expenses. The navy gave us all a per diem. I think it was thirty-five dollars a day. If you spent less, it was all profit.

On another level, there were Fred and I slowly circling each other. Certainly, in his case, not at all sure where this was all going, but not placing any obstruction in the path we had set out upon.

So many things could have been different. I could have been assigned to new duty immediately. Fred could have gotten a new assignment right away. The civilian officer could have pled his case again and less drunkenly and I could have gotten very distracted. He was in many ways a better choice. I'm sure he would have been very hot in bed. Not that Fred wasn't. But the officer was older. Knew more of life. I might be with him today if things had worked out differently. One always has to consider these possibilities. But such was not to be. We actually made a date to meet in a bar San Francisco. But he called and canceled. I never heard from him again. The feeling that I was playing a role in a scenario that I had in no way written continued. I was swept along. As you shall see.

Fred and Bill Cross the Sexual Barrier

I don't think it's easy to sleep with someone for the first time. I think it's darn hard. The first time may be the most exciting time but it certainly isn't the best time. When I run into those guys who only want to sleep with a man once and then that's it, I can't help but think they don't know what they're missing.

I don't think I ever stayed in a rooming house before I shared that room with Fred on Sacramento Street. The rooming house was in fact several houses. The other men from the *Henrietta Peabody* were in the main house where there was a dining room. Did they serve breakfast there? They must have. I'm sure I never ate there. Across the street was another building where people were housed, which had a television room in its basement.

Our building had the bleakness that only wooden houses in fog-bound cities can have. The sun is never blazing in San Francisco, you know. It always has a kind of aloofness. A feeling that "This is plenty enough sun for you. You're warm, quit complaining." But you never get so warm that it stays in your bones once the fog rolls in. The sun always seems to be a respite from the fog, even though the fog only rolls in for a few hours as the sun sets.

Romantic. Desperate. That's San Francisco. It's a town made for loneliness. You count yourself lucky if you've clawed some warmth and human affection for yourself out of the atmosphere. Scotland is like that, too. The climate has you always on edge, prepared to be chilly. There's never any overflow of sensuousness radiating from your body. It's absorbed immediately by the damp.

Our rooming house must have been a home at one time. A staircase ran steeply up from the front door, after climbing an equally steep flight of steps from the street.

On the street-level floor had been the kitchen and the dining room for the family who lived there. On the floor above, the one that the double Victorian front doors opened into, had certainly been sitting rooms. Rooms that friends were invited into. This must have been their original use. Above that had certainly been the master bedroom. This was our room. Narrow with the inevitable San Francisco bay window bulging toward the street. Those extra windows curving outward should have admitted more light. But it was dim and empty in the back of the room where the closets were. There were two beds. One against the hall wall, sideways. Fred took that. One with its head against the opposite wall, a bed that stood sideways to the bay windows. There was a bureau and a mirror in the corner beyond the head of Fred's bed.

I didn't really know what to do next. I had very little experience in the launching of an affair. I didn't know any of the phrases that I learned later, like, "Do you like to undress people?" Of course, you'd have to have had some experience to know if you like to undress people or not. So we talked a lot. We went out and had dinner at the little coffee shop on the corner. We came back. There were low lights in the room. Fred lay on his bed, head propped on one elbow. I lay on mine, looking at him, my head held up with my pillows against the wall. There were no headboards. There was no color in that room. Everything had been drained out of the much-washed mustard bedspreads, scuffed out of the machine-made oriental carpet. The walls were the color of old bones. But at night it was orange-yellow and black in that room. We each huddled in our little cave of light on our beds in the darkness of the room.

I think Fred did most of the talking. He told me about Kansas. About his mother, who stayed upstairs a lot. His brothers, hale and hearty fellows, neither of them married. His father, another hale and hearty fellow. Nothing really worked in that family but it didn't worry anyone because they knew no families where things worked. They knew no one who talked about what they thought.

Aside from the tractors and the electric lights swinging on a cord above the kitchen table, Fred and I had both been raised in the rural, provincial world that stretched back to the Puritans who stumbled off their ships, started planting corn, and never thanked the Indians for their help. I'm sure I quoted Thoreau and told Fred about people who lived "lives of quiet desperation." I think if Fred loved me it was because he had finally found someone he could talk to. Probably the second night of endless talk he got up from his bed and came to lie down across the foot of mine. I put my feet firmly against his thighs for warmth. I was nervous. Cold from nervousness. Cold from fear that finally some man was going to love me. Cold from fear of saying goodbye to a world that was entirely romantic fantasy and boyish sexual experimentation.

Fred pulled himself up beside me and took me in his arms. Very slowly our faces met. Slowly our cheeks lay beside each other. Slowly our lips crawled over each other. I love kissing and Fred was a well-qualified kisser.

I pressed my crotch against his. "No, no, we mustn't do that," he said. And returned to kissing me.

"Let's go to bed," I said, and got up and went to the closet to put on my pajamas. I wore pajamas. White ones with navy blue piping on the collar and pocket. Most of the officers wore pajamas. Boys were brought up wearing pajamas then. Sleeping in your underwear was all right aboard ship, but off duty you civilianized yourself at bedtime. Fred just pulled off his shirt, trousers, and socks. There he stood in his government issue white T-shirt and underdrawers with the little ties on the sides. He was robust. His chest and arms stretched the T-shirt into curves. His large thighs filled the legs of the white cotton shorts. He got into bed and pulled me to him.

Fred was big and he was firm but he wasn't hard. The long empty days of Guam when he'd spent a lot of time working out with weights had given him big biceps and a full chest, but they weren't like concrete. They were comfortable. Fred was really an easy man to sleep with. The easiest I've ever known. He liked to be all intermingled with my body when he slept. I liked being all intermingled with his body, but I didn't sleep. As I kissed him he responded to my pressing my groin against his. He pressed back. We were necking and dry-humping. That was what it was called. Nice girls didn't dryhump. Nor did they go in for heavy petting. Petting was running your hands over the other party's body. Heavy petting was running your hands over the other body's parts. I didn't touch Fred's penis, but both my pajamas and shorts closed loosely in the front. As we lay on our sides I pulled his shorts down to let his penis free and inserted it between my legs. He pulled it out immediately in alarm and said, "We have to go to sleep now."

Which we did somehow, in that narrowish bed not meant for two men, both over six feet.

When Fred said he was in love with me, I don't think he realized how this would manifest itself. And as I was to find out in our long conversations, he had never had a girlfriend over an extended period of time so that sexual experimentation could take place. He had had sexual intercourse with girls in Kansas. But just the "me on top, you on the bottom" kind of thing. He told me that he had met a woman in a bar while out drinking in San Francisco. She invited him up for a cup of coffee when they left the bar. In her apartment she immediately started undressing and Fred had said, "What about that cup of coffee?" She had said, "Huh? I don't even own a coffee pot."

That was the last time he had had sex before clambering into bed with me. For him this was something quite different. Hardly in a sexual category at all. This was in the love category. He was this creature that actually paid attention to me. He was well aware that my need for his love was great. As was his need for my attention. He sorely needed my focus upon him. I sorely needed to be fucked, and he came through for me.

How we spent that following day escapes me completely. I may very well have dragged him to the California Palace of the Legion of Honor. I was always very big on museums. They had a real honest-to-god Rodin statue in the courtyard of that big, out-of-place marble pile on the windy heights above the bay. Or that may have been a day we went to the movies in some great sprawling movie palace on Market Street. To see something with Susan Hayward.

After the movie we truly had sex. That night I don't think there was a lot of fooling around. We got into bed and took the pajamas and T-shirt and shorts off immediately. He placed himself between my legs and went at it. From his big, pale, cushiony body pounding on top of me, I came when he did. We kissed through the entire act.

But how curious that when I went down the hall to use the bath-room (I had to urinate furiously) I looked at myself in the mirror over the sink in that criminal light, all heavy shadows under the eyes, and said, "At least I'm not in love with him." I said it out loud. And went back in and crawled into his arms, waiting there to receive me.

He said into my ear, "This must be love when we can get into each other's arms right after having done it." He held me tightly as he slept. And I fell in love with him because he was in love with me.

To San Diego

I cried a lot in the taxi to the air terminal. People didn't take taxis to the airport in those days. We took taxis to an air terminal, checked our luggage there, and piled into a bus with other passengers. Fred was impressed.

I was probably very tired. We had fucked a lot in those days in the rooming house waiting for our next assignments. Gone to the theater and the ballet. Shopped. I bought Fred a maroon cashmere sweater and some matching socks. Maria Tallchief had danced the Swan Princess in the New York City Ballet's one-act version of *Swan Lake*. I knew little about ballet, but we had good seats and were quite close to her pale, powdered suffering. It seemed to be very much about how I felt. My prince had been assigned to a transport ship to Japan. I was going to an admiral's staff in San Diego. Would we ever see each other again? Did he want to? Actually, did I want to?

Fred said later, "You needed affection and I needed attention." That was true. I needed a lot of affection. I used to push him away from me in bed so I could see his strong, full, hairless white chest and strong arms, propping him off my body as he probed between my legs. Before we left that room he discovered a few hairs emerging on that bulging, marblelike chest. "I must be becoming a man," he said. I told him I loved his arms and he replied, "I love you, but not for your arms or anything like that."

He loved me because he was to leave the navy soon and was lost. I was willing to talk endlessly about what he should do. Should he go to college? Where? What should he study? What should he plan to become? We discussed his life endlessly as we lay on a narrow bed in that ugly, high-ceilinged rooming house room in the gray light of San Francisco. And he actually became what he planned to become.

By being locked in his arms the better part of every day, I was moving past the desperate need to simply be in bed with a man. I was beginning to feel something for him beyond fantasy. I always thought Fred was a better person than I was. He wasn't homosexual but simply acting upon his impulse to love this person who was truly interested in him. He wasn't living out a lifetime of saturation in Hollywood movies and *Saturday Evening Post* stories, as I was. What he was doing was real. What I was doing was largely acting out images and words I had seen and read. But he was becoming more real for me.

One evening as we were getting ready to go out, Fred came from the bathroom down the hall. I was wearing a seersucker bathrobe from Brooks Brothers, reaching up into a closet near the door. He pulled me to him from behind, held me close, and buried his face in my freshly washed neck. I didn't really know how to respond. I wrapped my arms backward around him and held him as closely as I could. It wasn't sexual. It was intimacy and it was us. It surprised me.

Another afternoon I was lying in his lap. He was sitting with his back against the wall, holding me as I lay across the bed. I looked up at him and lifted my eyebrows to make my face look smoother. He reached across the bed to where he kept a pad and pencil and wrote a poem, which he immediately showed me.

> Don't ever doubt.
> The love we bear
> And the love we share
> Is ours forever.

I felt something of an impostor. I was the one so infatuated with love, love. But he was the one who actually felt things more deeply.

I memorized that poem and used to recite it to myself long after I discovered I had it wrong. I found it later among the letters and notes Fred had written me, and it was in fact:

> Don't despair, don't
> Ever, ever doubt.
>
> Look deep, deep
> In my eyes and my
> Heart

The love you seek
And my love for you
Is there.

Unmeasurable,
And inexpressible
In words but
There, always
There, forever

This was quite an unusual effort for Fred. He wrote it down like this in its entirety sitting on the bed with me in his arms in a few moments. We had gotten ourselves mired in something deep. He always felt later that I had mired him in it. But I don't think that was the case.

My most vivid memory of all is of the afternoon we went to a matinee movie. We climbed into the balcony and, stepping through a velvet drapery, found ourselves plunged into blackness. Instinctively our hands went out and clasped together. I hadn't reached out first, although I was slightly behind Fred. We had both reached for each other simultaneously.

I suppose these are the things you forget when you fall out of love. You forget those moments of instinctively reaching for each other that have nothing to do with role-playing.

This was what I was crying about as I left for the plane. But once on the plane my spirits lifted and I wondered if there were going to be any good-looking young officers on the admiral's staff in San Diego.

When I reported for duty there, I discovered the naval base was on North Island, which filled the greater part of San Diego Bay. The town on the island was called Coronado. A ferry carried cars as well as passengers across to this very nearby island. The part of the base I reported to was for the amphibious force, located down the long strand of sandy beach that reached south from the island toward Tijuana on the Mexican border.

Big struggles can be easily forgotten. Mine was to decide whether I would live in the bachelor officers' quarters (the BOQ) on the base or take an apartment in town. Instinctively I opted for the BOQ, as my whole life had been spent either with my brothers or in a fraternity at school and then in a naval training school and aboard ship. I had never been alone. What would I do alone?

The weedy, pale little junior-grade lieutenant who reported in at the same time I had wanted me to share a room with him. I realized that if I didn't live alone in Coronado, my love affair with Fred was truly and definitely over. He would never be able to visit me in the BOQ. Enlisted men and officers did not socialize.

A boy I knew from home who had gone through naval officer training with me was stationed at the base, living off-base with his very pretty wife, a girl I also knew from home. His wife, Angela, found me an apartment not far from where they lived in Coronado. I could take a bus from there to the base every morning with no difficulty. I was terrified.

The apartment was one room with a sleeper sofa and a small kitchenette and bathroom. But rather charming. Pickled pecky cypress covered the walls. There was a built-in bookcase filled with books, a nice rug, good upholstery on the chairs and the couch. Pleasant light from low lamps. A very large walled garden was private to the apartment. A big banana tree dominated the garden and there were a table and chairs for dining outdoors. It was certainly the most glamorous environment I had ever lived in as my own dwelling. But what was I going to do there all by myself every evening and two long days every weekend?

This is perhaps the reason people marry the wrong person, go into a monastery, remain in the military. What was I going to do all by myself? I feared it greatly. So what did I do? I read.

As a fast reader, I probably read a book a day. Certainly I tore through all the books in the little library on the wall over my bed. I also discovered there was an excellent library on the base and carried away armloads of books from there every week. After a month I had beaten it. I learned to live alone. It was like kicking a drug habit, or learning a foreign language. I was free. I was no longer dependent on the presence of other people. And I could explore the world myself. Wanting to be with Fred led me to learn to be myself.

I was a cryptographic officer for the admiral at the base. That was what I had been trained to be aboard the aircraft carrier and what I had done at Bikini. There was very little to be done on a shore base. Most messages were coming in without being coded. And in-the-clear messages didn't pass through our offices.

My duties largely involved going once a week to the main cryptographic office in downtown San Diego and drawing out the new codes for the week ahead. Codes were changed every seven days and the previous codes had to be burned. For this trip I was driven in a limousine or a Jeep by an enlisted driver and wore a sidearm to shoot anyone who might try to steal the codes from me. I would have been useless in a war, as I couldn't really consider the enemy to be horrible people. But anyone who attacked me was going to get it and get it good.

I had a fellow officer who accompanied me on these sorties on the ferry to San Diego. In the back of the limousine he told me at great length about dreaming of a pistol in his hand that just wouldn't shoot. I had never studied psychology but I thought I could figure that one out. What his wife thought of that bulletless pistol we never discussed.

He was soon replaced with a WAVE officer. What kind of shot she was I never knew, as much of our time was spent discussing the malady she had on her feet. Some kind of creeping crud. It was crawling over both feet and often she came to work with them swathed in gauze and wearing Kleenex boxes.

Estelle was married to an enlisted man (at least you could marry one even if you couldn't socialize with them) and I always had some feeling that the disturbed feet were caused by some deep-seated sexual misunderstanding at home. I never met the husband. He wasn't stationed on our base though they lived together in town. Either she didn't want to run away and thought he might, or perhaps she felt she had really put her foot in it. I never counseled her on the subject, although I certainly thought about it.

A rather cheery, chunky new junior officer named Al had turned up on base, and he rented a ramshackle old house directly across the street from me. He was an aficionado of airline stewardesses and his house was filled with guests frequently. I hung around over at his house from time to time. We were both very fond of a lithograph that hung on the wall of his living room depicting a young lady pulling her skirts high to avoid any contact with a basket of peaches that she had dropped at her feet. We always called it *Splashing Peaches.* Al had a refined sense of humor despite his taste for stewardesses.

I also learned to cook for myself in my enforced isolation. At a nearby meat market I told the butcher I would buy what he suggested if he would tell me how to prepare it. My recipe for calf's liver wrapped in bacon comes from him and it is a good one.

I bought a bicycle and pedaled down to the beach on the weekend. It was near the great white heap of the Coronado Beach Hotel, which figured in the movie *Some Like It Hot* and was also where Wallis Warfield Simpson was first presented to the Prince of Wales, later the Duke of Windsor.

There was a small bar on the nearby main street of Coronado where I would go with Al and his friends occasionally, too. It was called something like the Honolulu Grill and had small windows lining the room with views of tropical sites. Regularly it would thunder and lightning and rain in these small apertures. It had a hint of excitement about it but was nothing compared to the Tonga Room at the Fairmont Hotel in San Francisco, where there was an all-out storm over the central pool that often drove the orchestra to seek shelter. The orchestra floated on a raft in the center of the pool and frequently the staff forgot to pull it out of the way of the stormy weather, which occurred every hour on the hour. Later I found in New York that the Menemsha Grill had the same storms in tiny windows, but these were over views of the Maine coast.

One night as I came home late I was drawn to the mailbox, although I had already collected the mail once for the day. In it was a thick letter from Fred, mailed from Japan. It was everything you would want in a letter from a distant lover. He gave the date of his arrival in San Francisco. I was feeling very much like sleeping with him again and made plans to fly up to meet the ship, whose arrival was not too many days off.

Coffee Dan

I was sexually attacked when I went back to San Francisco to meet Fred. Not by Fred. It really came as a big surprise to me.

I took a room in the same rooming house where Fred and I had been before. He had stayed at this place for some time while waiting for the assignment, which had sent him to Bikini. His roommate while he had stayed there was a young man called Coffee Dan. Dan, really, I suppose.

There was a kind of hip coffee shop in San Francisco at that time called Coffee Dan's. Thus the nickname. There were a number of those small nightclub/bar/coffee shops around the city then. The Hungry I, where Mort Sahl worked as a stand-up comic in his V-necked sweater holding a newspaper, the Purple Onion, the Fat Black Pussycat. San Francisco was the happening place then, much more avante-garde than New York.

I ran into Coffee Dan when I checked in, and he suggested that we have something to eat together. He was a small, sallow, thin guy with, surprisingly, gray-blue eyes. They made him look like a hungry wolf.

I wasn't really concentrating on Dan. I was very excited about Fred returning the next day, so when Dan asked me to come back to his room I thought little about it. He sat on a chair. I lolled on his daybed and laughed a lot. It was probably the lolling that did it. When I was in cryptographic school at the Del Monte Hotel in Monterey, one of the other junior officers saw me lie down on my bed and said, "You can't even lie down without being glamorous, can you?"

Suddenly Dan said, "And I have other interests, too." In a flash he locked the door, turned out the light, and fell on top of me. Dan had finally gotten my attention. I was stunned and got out from under him, turned on the light, and unlocked the door just as rapidly as he had done the reverse. At the door I said, "You're making a mistake." And rushed to my room, which was in the adjoining house.

I sat on the side of the bed. I was twice as big as Coffee Dan, but he had frightened me. There was a silly little person inside of me who had been scared to death. I was still shaking when Dan knocked on the door. I didn't answer when he called my name. Somehow he knew I was there and said through the door, "I'm sorry, but if I'm wrong you should be careful. Everybody's talking." I went to bed feeling sick and alone in an ugly boardinghouse room.

I don't know who "everybody" could have been. The other sailors who had come back with us from Bikini and had stayed at the rooming house had long since dispersed to new duty. What if someone there had gone to the bother of reporting their suspicions to the navy? What if I were queried about my relationship with Fred? Of course I would have denied it. And denied him. Perhaps I was running along a chancy precipice, perhaps not. But those were not thoughts that concerned me. I seemed to have been waiting a very long time to really be in love with another man. And miraculously, Fred with his big, blond body and strong arms had appeared. That was all I could think about, all that concerned me. I was far from having casual sex with Coffee Dan, who probably had a sinewy body and a big winkie—that kind of man usually does. The very idea of it left me in shock.

Our Romance

I was still in distress the next morning. I needed to flee to Fred as quickly as I could. I took a taxi through the San Francisco morning to the pier. Only San Francisco has these mornings. The light was pale and flat and the buildings looked washed out against the light blue sky. It was cool in the fresh, light smoky salt-smelling morning as I walked down the pier.

Relatives were clustered here and there on the pier also, which was really a big open-sided warehouse jutting out into the bay. The ship emerged quickly from the haze on the water and tied up shortly after I got there. Its side loomed far above me. Ships always seem much larger when you're beside them than when you're on them.

Many of the ship's company were at the rail shouting down to their friends and family, but no Fred. He was probably on duty, I thought. I walked back and forth for perhaps an hour beside the ship.

These things pass through your mind as you wait for someone on a ship. Perhaps they aren't on the ship. They have fallen overboard, the family has been notified, you have been left in the dark. The family doesn't even know of your existence. Your lover is, in fact, on the ship but has had a change of heart and doesn't want to see you anymore. He's hoping you'll give up and go away.

I felt his eyes on me and looked up. He wasn't at the rail but standing back against the bulkhead under the overhang of the deck above. He had evidently been studying me. His pale blue eyes looked dark and sad. He wasn't smiling. When our eyes met it was like putting a wet finger on a faulty light switch. He moved slowly to the rail and called down in a low voice that he couldn't leave the ship until noon. And disappeared. All the other families and friends had gone away, too. Gone home to wait there for their loved ones.

All alone in my raincoat and gray flannel slacks, I moved restlessly back and forth in the cavernous shed of the pier until he came down the plank in his snug navy uniform, stretched over those thighs and that full torso of a Greek river god.

We walked together to a taxi without saying much. Obviously I wasn't going to embrace him. We didn't even hold hands in the taxi. I knew all the romantic clichés of how lovers comported themselves, but I felt shy about doing them with Fred. It was he, in fact, who initiated our intimate behavior in the months that lay ahead.

At the rooming house we went straight to our room and without consulting one another gravely undressed. Fred was in before me. Naked with an erection, I looked at him and he opened his big arms to me. He pulled me to him and we immediately began making love with no preliminaries. From the first, we made love with him placing himself between my held-together legs. The Greeks had a name for this kind of lovemaking. "Between the femurs" or something like that. He came like that and I had my orgasm from his body pressing against me. It was a very pure love, our love. His penis became chafed and I began using some hair pomade between my legs to smooth the passage. The idea of greasing up, putting towels down, the paraphernalia of experienced lovers we would have found offensive. Then we would have been practiced seekers of sexual pleasure. What we had was the inevitable necessity of two people engulfed in love. Fred wasn't in love with male bodies—he was in love with me. I was more knowledgeable but I wasn't going to call it to his attention that what we were doing was called homosexuality.

When we finished our lovemaking, he sat on the edge of the bed naked and said, "I just wish I could take you away to a desert island somewhere so I wouldn't have to think about the rest of it."

Fred's ship was going to be in port for a week or more and I had taken some days of leave. So we were able to be together all day, every day. We were in bed most of it. I put out of my mind that "people" at the rooming house were talking about us. I told him about my run-in with Coffee Dan and he seemed reluctant to believe it. "I roomed with him for almost a month and nothing like that ever happened," he said, looking at me suspiciously. I knew so little about lovers and how they were expected to act that I let the subject drop without defending myself or accusing him of naïveté. We never ran into Dan and there was little reason to think about it more.

For some reason I decided to take Fred to Monterey to visit my oldest brother and his family—Carmel, actually, where my bother was living, over the hill from Monterey. Surely we must have had the money to go away together to a beach resort. I guess we just didn't know how to go about it.

My brother Ransome had been in the navy for thirteen years and he was only one rank ahead of me. No wonder he didn't like me. Furthermore, he had never been outside the federal waters of the United States and I was a veteran of fourteen crossings of the Pacific, had visited Hong Kong and Guam, and had just returned from the hydrogen bomb test at Bikini. There was a lot not to like. He said nothing when I turned up with an enlisted man, but I could tell he thought it was bizarre. But he was one of the founders of the school of "Don't ask anything or you may hear something you don't like." Many a boat went unrocked by old Ransome. Maybe that's why he had chosen to become a submariner.

His wife, Marie, was only a few years older than I was, and I had known her since she was eighteen. The fact that Fred was an enlisted man registered nothing with her. They were expecting their third child soon and she was doing a lot of sleeping and resting. She settled Fred into the guest room at the head of the stairs over the garage and I was put on the folding bed in the living room. I kept my clothes in the guest room so there was occasionally time for a little hurried hanky-panky up there, but not much.

I took Fred to Point Lobos the first day. There is a little cove there where the waves come crashing up. A small gray house stands under a very large tree overlooking this cove. In early whaling days they dragged whales here and boiled up their blubber. I guess the whalers lived in the little house. Perhaps the tree wasn't even there then. Or much smaller. A woman was standing at the door of the house when we drove past. Perhaps the ranger of this little park lived there. I hoped that she loved him very much. It was the perfect place to be stranded with someone you were crazy about.

Looking back, I was very insistent on having sex with Fred when I wanted it, although he sometimes surprised me by launching foreplay in public places. And I could be dismissive when I wasn't in the mood. Now, of course, I wish I had given him whatever he wanted physically, whenever he wanted it. But I had yet to learn to give someone else pleasure, whether it was a pleasure for me or not.

The paths that wind around the cliffs of Point Lobos are narrow and drop directly into the water beating against the rocks below. Teal birds were dipping for fish below our feet. The path crossed a long slope of blowing gray-green grass and dipped under a very low-slung pine. Under the branches I pulled Fred to me and kissed him. There was always something mournful in Fred's eyes when he looked at me. He loved me but he didn't really want to. I loved him and I wanted to. There was a big difference.

He kissed me lightly, as if he was just reminding himself that I was there. Once in bed he had said, "I know what gets you excited" and kissed me with a lot of passion. He was right. He was being careful now.

I think we both knew there was something fragile about our love. We watched over it carefully, sensing that every time we separated it could become something we had both only dreamed. Since then I've learned that it's very rare for both people to lose themselves to love. More often there is one who keeps a part of the mind aloof, thinking, "Do I really want to go through with this? Can I do better than this? Am I only in this for the sex?" Fred said often, "We must remember this." But as it turned out, I was better than he at remembering.

The next day, while the children took their naps, Fred and I went to the beach. In Carmel this is just down at the bottom of the street. Ransome was at the Navy Graduate School over the hill in Monterey. Marie was planning to nap, too.

We went in the freezing cold water and came out to lie on our towels. We didn't talk very much. Fred rolled over on his side and, propping his head on one hand, looked at me. He said nothing. But the look said he really needed to fuck me and he needed to do it now. "Let's go home," I said, and we walked back up the hill, went in the house where everyone was sleeping, and went straight to the guest room. We pulled off our swimsuits, and I lay down on the single bed in its dark green bedspread. Fred closed the door and lay down on me. What we were doing was dangerous, as Marie was quite capable of coming up the stairs and throwing open the door to see what was going on. I held Fred very tightly, as he needed this and had instigated it. He was leaving the next day to go back to his ship. Why was I staying behind at my brother's? I should have gone back to San Francisco with him, seen him off and gone back to San Diego, even before my leave was up. We transit from one kind of life to another in bits and pieces.

I took Fred to his early train in Monterey the next morning. It was foggy going over the hill. At the station we sat in the car. I held his hand and I cried. My window was open, and a man suddenly put his head in, saw our linked hands, and said, "Your lights are on." I thanked him. Maybe he hadn't seen the tears streaming down my face.

Maybe I should admit here that I was pretty lost without Fred. I knew there were other homosexuals but I had never seen one I could imagine being linked with. The boys I'd slept with in my hometown were history. I wasn't going to be seeing them again. So where did that leave me? I was waiting for Mr. Right and suddenly he had appeared in the person of Mr. Frederick Poe Jorgensen. It was pretty uncanny. At one point later I clung to him and said, "Don't leave me right now, Fred. Not quite yet." But not this foggy morning beside the train track in Monterey. Do you remember that scene in *East of Eden* when James Dean approaches his mother, who is a whorehouse madam, in the fog? It was just like that. What is it about the northern California coast that lends itself to dramatic emotions?

So Fred left. I stayed a couple more days with Ransome and Marie and the kids. We had kept the room at the rooming house in San Francisco and Fred stayed there, leaving the day before I arrived. Again, why wasn't I with him? Who knows? I was staying there myself overnight before the morning flight to San Diego.

That room was purgatory. So ugly. So bleak. It was like being trapped in an Andrew Wyeth painting. I just stood and looked about, my bag at my feet, wondering if I was going to be able to stand it.

Then suddenly I knew. I went over to the bureau by the window and opened the top drawer. I would never have put any clothes in there. But for some reason I pulled it open and found the letter Fred had left for me there. Lying face up, not folded, in that tiny sort-of-awkward handwriting of his. He must have known how horrible it would be in that room for me alone. He wrote a letter about how much he loved me. And he signed it, "Te Amo, Fred." Fred was lost and I was leading him somewhere else. I was lost and he was holding me in his arms.

I must have been more uneasy about incriminating evidence than I remember being, because once in San Diego and having read it many times, I tore his letter into tiny pieces. It was the only letter of his I ever did this to. I then searched in the wastebasket and found the scrap with the "Te Amo, Fred" on it, and this I carried with me for many years. It's still somewhere. In a little silver box or in the bottom of a jewelry case somewhere.

I resumed my silly life in San Diego. My *real* life was Fred. My make-believe life was being a junior officer on the admiral's staff on North Island in San Diego Bay. I hung around with my *Splashing Peaches* friend from across the street. We even went out on dates with some very nice girls. The kind of girls who didn't, or at least in those days didn't, think it was strange that you didn't want to kiss them good night.

One of them said to me one day when I wearing gray flannel shorts that I had cut down from some slacks, "I wish I had long beautiful legs like yours." I said nothing. No one ever told me I had beautiful legs before, although there were to be many compliments in the years ahead. Perhaps ten years later my friend Vivian wired me one day when I had taken a new job in New York, "When you're tall, blond, and have wonderful legs, what can go wrong?" By that time all the things that can go wrong seemed all right to me.

Fred's trips to Japan on his cargo ship took close to two months there and back. So I couldn't count on getting letters for some five weeks. But one did arrive. In that same small, disjointed handwriting Fred told me that he felt our relationship (he didn't use that word; no one did yet) was wrong. He did not plan to sleep with me anymore. He had even gone to a Japanese whorehouse to prove something to himself. He would be back soon.

WAITING

No Sex Please, We're Sailors

The surprising thing in my letters to my mother that I wrote at this time is that I never mention Fred. They prattle on. Really prattle. They talk a lot about my plans to enter the diplomatic corps. They refer to God a lot, too. But all during the period of being at Bikini I never mention Fred.

I do mention him finally after the incident in Hawaii but mention it as though I have been some kind of instructor and spiritual guide to him. There is no indication of the emotional and sexual tailspin I was in. I even mention girls I am going out with. My poor mother.

When Fred's ship came in to San Francisco the second time, I was there to meet it. I was frantic at the idea that he was not going to sleep with me anymore. I had a lot of martinis during lunch, and we headed for the de Young Museum in Golden Gate Park. We had to change buses several times and each time we did, I dragged Fred into a bar at the bus stop and had another martini. I was really drunk by mid-afternoon. By the time we got back to our hotel room, in what was really a rather good hotel, I was sobbing. I fell on the bed crying. I suppose I was pretty uncontrollable. Poor Fred. He took my clothes off and fucked me properly from the front. The first time we had ever done that. When I asked him about that later he said, "I had to do something to calm you down."

We fell asleep and I woke up about an hour later. His heavy body was still on top of me. He was sound asleep. His weight on my spread thighs made it difficult to get out from under him, and I could hardly walk on my numb legs to the bathroom. On the toilet I let his sperm drop out of me. And in the bathtub I had filled with warm water, I sat and soaked my sore rectum. The water was hot, the bathroom was cold, the horrible gray late afternoon light of San Francisco filled the room. Fred was asleep naked on the bed in that same awful light in the next room.

When Fred woke up, we got dressed and went out to dinner. I got drunk all over again and threw up in the gutter in front of the Fat Black Pussycat. I was disgusting.

We never discussed this day and night in San Francisco until much later. I flew back to San Diego the next morning and resumed my life as the head cryptographic officer on the admiral's staff. The low dun buildings down the Silver Strand from Coronado were very undistinguished, as was the low dun room that was my office. I didn't know it at the time, but the base strongly resembled Hollywood studios. Except that nothing very exciting was going on inside.

In town, my off-hours life continued to be reminiscent of college, except for the fact that I lived alone. My pal across the street and I continued to eat meals together, went to the movies, and sometimes went out on dates with those girls I had no intention of even kissing.

In my own little apartment complex were some rather complex people. A young single woman who lived across the lawn and upstairs told me over a cup of coffee that she had gone off a cliff in a car twice in her life. The first time she was a child with her parents, and the parents had been killed. On the Pacific Coast Highway. The second time had been more recent, with herself at the wheel. Again the Pacific Coast Highway. I had seen the remains of the cars at the foot of the cliffs near Big Sur and was both fascinated and vaguely ill at the idea of going off a cliff in a car. I asked her point-blank what it felt like. She said she didn't remember the first fall, but of the second one said, "It was very noisy." I hadn't thought of that. Of the car scraping and turning and bounding as it falls down the cliff face. I had a great deal of admiration for this plain-faced girl who drank a lot of coffee and smoked a lot of cigarettes and was very nervous underneath her dead-pan calm. Now I think she probably longed to be a lesbian underneath the ingrained shock of her plunges. I hope it happened.

Retired Admiral Saltonstall and Mrs. Saltonstall did not long to become lesbians. They didn't long to be anything. They lived next door to me on the ground floor facing the lawn and were supreme Bostonians, totally out of place in San Diego and happy to be so. They were both tall and thin and white haired, she a little more than he in all three categories. I liked the commander because one day he said to me in the garden, "God knows what went on in the Pacific. God and General MacArthur."

Mrs. Staltonstall asked me one day when we were chatting at her door if I had ever considered the ministry. I seemed to be such a fine young man. "You've only seen my good side," I said.

Fred had been planning a two-week leave with me in San Diego, and when we parted in San Francisco we didn't discuss whether it was still on or not. From Japan I got a letter that he was still coming and that he still believed we should not be sleeping together. Men didn't. Men shouldn't. It was wrong, wrong, wrong. I resigned myself to his decision.

Some Men Who Slept with Other Men, No. 1*

I SLEPT WITH GEORGE WASHINGTON

I know you have many questions. The first one, of course, is, "What about the false teeth?" You have to remember that George was relatively young when I slept with him. Or maybe I just didn't notice. And your second question will be, "Isn't it kind of unlikely, two generals sleeping together?" If you would think a moment of Alexander le Grand, Alexander the Great as you say, *all* the generals were sleeping together.

But I do understand your point of view. You also have to recall that I was but twenty-three when I came to America from France. And I had a very fresh complexion. You would not think anything of the sort from paintings of me when I was older. But I was young. I was from the court of Louis XVI. The generals in the French army were ancient and there were no wars. Soldiers are like anyone else. If you want to do business, you must go where the business is. And that was in the newly formed United States. They needed help. I needed a career. So we made a deal, as you would say nowadays.

Very honestly, I was not made a general because I slept with George. I slept with George because I wanted to. I know; all whores say that. But let's be honest. Whoring has many faces. It's just a matter of getting what you want. If you are satisfied to not get what you want, I hope it's also some satisfaction to know that you are not a whore. I never found it a problem. Only people who compliment themselves that they are not whores see it as a problem.

---

*I wrote this for Fred to reassure him that men had slept with other men, historically.

Louis XVI liked the Americans. More, he hated the English and couldn't bear the idea of their hanging onto the colonies. Particularly when all we had was that enormous stretch of tundra to the north. And God knows what kinds of desert wastes beyond the Mississippi.

But it was my idea to go. I got an audience with Louis. Our fathers actually had known each other rather well. He was enthusiastic in every way that I should go. And he was tired of my constantly importuning him for something to do around the court. I'm sure he thought that the Indians might kill me, or the British, and either way I was out of his wig, as we used to say then. He was never going to make me a general, and Washington was, so I had to go.

I could tell the moment I met General Washington that he fancied me. You always *can* tell. "You must pay with your purse or your person," as the old adage goes.

There really wasn't any negative to the situation. What was he going to do if he didn't get me into bed? Send me back to France? He wasn't such a *cocotte* as all that. He was actually quite attractive, George, aside from that habit of pinching his lips together so you couldn't see his bad teeth. I noticed the Empress Josephine did exactly the same thing later. Too bad they never met. They could have. I would have loved to have seen the two of them together, talking through those mouths like scarcely opened purses.

No, George had his good points. Physically he was very tall, you know. Over six feet. I was only five feet, six inches tall, which was quite normal for those times. In bed with George there wasn't a lot of room for anyone else. You must think me facetious, but actually I was in bed with him any number of times. So much for soldiers' lodgings. You must have noticed all those houses with signs saying, "George Washington slept here." They never mention that he wasn't alone a lot of the time. In those awful Gilbert Stuart paintings the artist made him look a lot like a sheep. The white wig, I imagine. Actually he never wore a wig or powdered his hair except for very formal occasions. He had nice brown hair and a lot of it. And he had that kind of meaty English yeoman kind of face. He was English, of course. But totally. The Washingtons were an old English family, if you care about that kind of thing. But no title, of course.

De toute façon, I knew what I was doing. I had been very well trained. And I was courageous. Courage is something like being a good shot. Or being able to run fast. Some men have it. Some men don't. And whether you like to sleep with other men or not has nothing to do with it. Ridiculous, isn't it, this idea that men who like to sleep with other men are like women? It's not easy to be brave when you're wearing eighteen yards of cloth, but I have known many women who were extremely courageous and had very little fear for their own welfare. You must remember, I lived through the French Revolution later.

George had plenty of courage. And he was a very decent sort. Very decent. You'd be surprised how many people are not. Aaron Burr, for example. He would have screwed a goat. I've always been of two minds about him. He made an excellent self-presentation, but I always felt he knew who Number One was, and no one was going to get in the way. I knew Alexander Hamilton, too. Very handsome. I should add, very, very handsome. I always thought Burr killed him because he wanted him and could never get him. Not as desperate as all that, of course, but you know these things always play a part. And these were short men. Shorter than me. This, too, always plays a part.

George was big. Big in body and big in spirit, too. He really was a very nice man and a gentleman. He was really the only one who could have been the Father of His Country.

I'm not really avoiding the details. I'll get to that. Sometimes I was off with my troops on sorties and skirmishes of my own. Sometimes I was in Washington's camp with many other officers and aides-de-camp. And we were always on the move. *Mon Dieu,* I must have slept in several hundred different private homes. Men always slept two or three to a bed in those days. No one was worried about sleeping with someone who would bugger him in the night. I assure you that if you are being buggered in the night and it doesn't wake you up, you are a very sound sleeper indeed.

No. George used to say, "Lafayette, why don't you share digs with me? I have many things to talk to you about and that way it will be easier . . ." And we would take our candles and mount the stairs. Those freezing rooms, those quilted counterpanes, the frost on the glass, the piss frozen in the chamber pots under the bed. It was all quite normal but it wasn't a holiday, of that you can be quite sure. I think one reason George wanted to sleep with me was that I was French and I didn't have cold feet. You know, we *are* Romance language people. We have Mediterranean blood coursing through our veins. I am warm in bed. "A little furnace," my wife used to say. A little furnace that the Father of the United States of America used to warm himself at. I am proud to say I was only too glad to do it.

George was very affectionate. He liked to bundle. How times change. Now sex is very athletic. All the clothes have to be off. The bedcovers have to be off. Both parties energetically using their bodies to the maximum. Who said, "Like two maniacs struggling in the dark?" In the eighteenth century both parties were rarely entirely out of their clothing. You pulled a skirt up here, dropped the front of breeches down there and *eh, voila!* And in bed there was always the nightshirt. It would have to be very warm weather to go to bed without a nightshirt or a nightgown. Some men wore their shirts, but shirts were down to your knees then.

George would just cuddle and cuddle and cuddle until I would think, "Let's get this over with so I can get some sleep." So I would reach down and masturbate him until he came heavily and I would mop it up with the tails of his nightshirt and go to sleep. Sometimes he would provide the same service to me. He didn't want to kiss. Those teeth again, I suppose.

This was not a very major thing. We didn't ever talk about it. He was a reasonable man. When the war was over, all we foreigners were feted and dined about and then we returned to our own countries. I think he was just happy to have had some affection from someone he fancied. And when the war was over he set about running the country.

I didn't do anything that Martha couldn't have done, but I don't think she would have liked it. It was wise of George to have married her. She came with two children, so that part was out of the way. She was an excellent housekeeper. She ran Mount Vernon very efficiently.

When he said good-bye for the last time as I was leaving for my ship, George embraced me strongly, and I knew he had felt very much for me. People laugh and say, "He may have been the Father of His Country, but he never had children." But he had me. And that counts for something.

The Marquis de Lafayette

The Two-Week Leave

There is a mini eclipse when a plane passes overhead and cuts between you and the sun. There is a wink of shadow. That is my story with Fred. A wink of shadow. But it was more than a wink to me.

Later in New York after my career in the theater, when I working in public relations, was in my early thirties, and fancied myself on the glittering front edge of youth and beauty and sexual adventurousness and desirability, I told a friend about Fred. He said scornfully, "Every gay guy has a story like that." It made me very unhappy to have my great romance denigrated in that way. Which is probably why I didn't sleep with that guy. So much for being a smart-ass.

When Fred called from San Francisco and said he was on his way to San Diego, I resigned myself to the fact that we weren't going to sleep together. If that was the way he wanted it, that was the way it would be. I was still very much a nice young man then. A nice boy, really. I'd slept with a number of boys through the years, but that wasn't love. Now I felt a novice. I wanted so much to be loved. To be rescued from the falsity of planning a sensible career, letting my mother think I would be married someday, talking and acting as though I was going to have a nice bourgeois life. Ye gods, in letters to my mother I even suggest that perhaps I would return to college and plan a career as an English teacher in Michigan so I could be near the family. What could I have been thinking? Fred saved my ass from all that. He loved me. I loved him. It was possible. What the rest of my life would be like hardly mattered. It had become clear to me what my priorities were.

Fred arrived in civvies, walking over from the ferry with his suitcase. I had sent him a map of how to find my apartment. I fixed supper for him and we ate in the greenery-choked garden in front of my apartment under the banana tree. When it came time to go to bed, I unfolded the bed. Got out the pillows and blankets and got in. From the darkened room I could see Fred in the bathroom. I had given him my pale blue cotton stretch pajamas, something like the running suits you see everywhere today, with knit cuffs and neck and a stretch waistband. When he turned away from the sink after brushing his teeth, I could see he had a hard-on. It poked the blue stretch fabric out very strongly in front of his crotch. He turned out the light and came into the room and fell heavily on top of me and on the bed and started kissing me. He wanted to fuck and I hadn't coaxed or cried him into it. What a relief.

Sleeping with Fred was like sleeping with a big, blond pile of cement. Warm, soft cement. He was heavy. I pulled that pair of blue jersey pajamas off him and started licking his body. I had always kissed and licked him a lot. He loved that. He liked having the nipples on his large rounded pectoral muscles sucked. Sometimes I would slop back and forth between the both of them until he was panting. This night I licked down his body and around the base of his cock. I licked his thighs, too. He had a light brown birthmark about the size of a postage stamp on the left one. I licked there, too, although I couldn't see it in the darkness. I went back to his cock and licked up the base and slipped it into my mouth. He let me suck it for a moment and then pulled me up and kissed me very thoroughly on the mouth. A mouth that had just contained his cock. We had crossed the lovers' mucous membrane barrier together. His mucous membranes were my mucous membranes from that point on. There are other kinds of closeness than talking about your feelings. He turned me over and climbed on me, fucking me from the back. He pulled my face around so that he could kiss me at the same time.

We fucked a lot for the rest of the two weeks he was with me. Every day and sometimes twice a day. We took a shower together in the afternoon after coming back from the beach. We fell to the floor of the shower with the water pounding down on us, but there was no way to really connect genitally. The little white tile room was too small. We went to the couch.

Because one could peer into the room from the courtyard, we put a towel down beside the end of the couch out of view from the window. We had to put our feet in the open door of the closet but that was fine.

I went to the base every day during the week and left Fred to sleep late and amuse himself. Sometimes I could come home from the base and we could have lunch together. Although Fred never wore his uniform, it was somehow clearly understood by all the navy-related folks in the apartment complex that he was an enlisted man. Mrs. Saltonstall said, "You are so nice to provide a place for an enlisted man to spend his leave. He must be enjoying your company." Her manner couldn't have been kinder, but it was clearly a warning that people had noticed.

I had had my mother send me my Billie Holiday records, and I would sometimes play them after we had gotten into bed and turned the lights off. That probably hadn't gone unnoticed.

My *Splashing Peaches* friend from across the street had another young officer staying with him on leave and I suggested that he hang out with Fred a little bit during the day while the rest of us were at the base.

Which they did. One afternoon I got away early and Fred and I had ridden bikes down to the beach near the Coronado Hotel. Once back, as frequently happened, we started fooling around as we were pulling our suits off. I had gone into the bathroom to get some Vaseline to use between my legs. We weren't doing the entering thing regularly. I would get sore and we had to wait until I had gotten over it. Fred was sitting on the folded-out couch with his zipper-front trunks open and his penis out and upright where I had been fondling it. I had the draperies pulled, but there was still plenty of light in the room. There was a knock on the door. Fred stared at me.

I motioned him into the closet and pulled on a bathrobe. I messed up my hair and tried to look sleepy.

It was the ensign from across the street. I peered around the door so he wouldn't see my erection under my robe. "Hi," I said. "I was taking a nap." I didn't invite him in. Fred was standing right behind me in the open closet door, his large penis still protruding from the front of his shorts.

"Do you guys want to go to the beach?" he said, his little light blue eyes in his pale, pinched face clearly suspicious. About something. "Fred is already down there," I said, thinking fast. "I was so tired from all that carousing last night that I just had to lay down." He clearly didn't believe me but left. "Let's lie down on the floor," I said to Fred, "in case he comes back." Despite the interruption, we had rich thrusting and shoving on the floor with deep orgasms. I loved to have Fred fuck me. His cock wasn't above a normal size, but the heavy body behind it made it clear that I was really being fucked. And it was clear that Fred was really enjoying his two-week stint of daily fucking.

It was more than just the daily fucking. At a big party across the street in my fellow officer's house, Fred and I had been delegated to make sandwiches in the kitchen. I was leaning against the counter with Fred beside me buttering the spread-out pieces of sandwich bread. The house was full of people but there was no one else in the kitchen momentarily when he leaned over and kissed me. It surprised me. It was a chance I wouldn't have taken.

Fred fucked me in his sleep one night. I awoke and he was lying partially on me. I pulled him on top of me and put his erection between my legs. The next morning he said, "I wasn't even awake last night. I woke up just as I was coming." There was a faint tone of accusation in his voice.

Just when I was beginning to accept my role as the bad person who was luring him into homosexual sex, he would surprise me. We went to a restaurant in La Jolla one evening, across the bay. My friend from across the street drove with his airline stewardess friend beside him in the front seat. Fred and I were behind. Halfway there he put his hand in my crotch and started fingering me until I had an erection inside my pants. I felt him also and brought him up to a hard-on. While we were doing this, I repeatedly leaned forward and chatted brightly with the occupants of the front seat so they wouldn't have to turn around to talk. Fred had an inventive sexuality with me that he would unleash and then later dislike himself for. I stopped blaming myself.

One evening during his two-week leave I went to meet him coming back from the mainland. Why he had gone over to San Diego I don't know. Something about checking with his ship or perhaps checking when he would be discharged perhaps. We were both scheduled to get out of the navy in the spring. Dusk was settling over the garden and seeping indoors. I decided to walk toward the boat landing where he would be arriving by ferry. There were any number of different streets to take from my apartment to the landing but I wandered off instinctively. Within two blocks I saw him coming up the street in the now shadowy light. We met. We didn't kiss but we touched. And we walked home in the dark hand in hand. It's a very delicate thing, love. We were just two blokes who were kind of lost without each other. This kind of deep interweaving beneath the skin needs only sex as a kind of seal of approval. It was even more thrilling than orgasm, seeing him there, being able to touch him, to reassure myself that he did actually exist.

These things are so fragile that they are easily forgotten. And they were forgotten by Fred. But for a time we two vulnerable young men lived in a world of our own making within another world that was restrictive and threatening. I wonder if men fell in love with each other in concentration camps. They must have. There was that play *Bent,* wasn't there? The love we had for each other had to be reassuring because we had each found someone who cared for us in what was essentially the very uncaring gray metal structure of the navy.

With the young officer from across the street and his airline stewardess friend we took another car trip to Los Angeles to return the stewardess to her plane. It was the night before Fred was to leave. On the coastal highway the sun came flooding in over the waves as it headed for setting. I was exhausted. I had been going to the base every morning doing my cryptographic job and eating and laughing and fucking all night for two weeks. Fred was fine. He'd been sacking out on the sleeper sofa most of the day while I was out in my starched khakis keeping the admiral's communications in order.

I leaned my tired head on Fred's shoulder and he pulled me around so his arm was around my neck and my back was against his body, my head resting in the muscular curve of his shoulders and upper arm. He reached around to my face, which he couldn't see, and felt gently to see if my eyes were closed against the sun. Our friends in the front seat didn't seem to pay attention, but it wasn't exactly a naval regulation kind of cuddle. Again, I never would have crossed the border in public that would have called attention to our romance. Fred didn't seem to mind.

He was like some large, blond god who had drifted down from ancient times when Zeus could fall in love with Ganymede and that's just how it was. It was just one of the many things I loved about him. His air of being above reproach.

When we got home it was almost dawn. We made love violently and he perspired heavily, as though his whole body was crying.

I don't think Fred had had enough of me by the time he had to report back to his ship in San Francisco. Nor do I think he found himself bound any closer. I cried a lot the day he had to leave. He was seated in the little armchair in my wood-paneled room. I was kneeling in front of him, pressed between his spread legs, holding him very closely and sobbing. He was getting used to this and I think he liked it.

The phone rang and I got up to answer it. I would answer the phone in the middle of a mud slide. It was my cousin Betty in San Diego.

"You sound terrible. What's wrong?" she said.

"I have a really bad cold," I lied. I tried to sound more cheerful. I hung up. I went back to Fred, but the peak was over. In his uniform with his ditty bag on his shoulder, he must have walked down to catch the ferry over to San Diego. I must have walked with him to the boat. But I don't remember this. I am sure I didn't go with him to the airport. I wonder why now. No one did in those days.

Song

She was just a sailor's sweetheart
And she loved her sailor lad.
Though his first love was the navy
He was all she ever had.
Now she still believes in sailors
And she's true to the red, white, and blue.
And although she's barred
From the navy yard
She still loves her sailor boy . . . absolutely!

Terrible Weekends

The enigmatic Fred, after two weeks of lovemaking and a certain amount of crying on my part, departed. This time he didn't write from Japan to say he felt we shouldn't sleep together anymore. He wrote a noncommittal little note and was vague about when his ship was returning to San Francisco. He, of course, underestimated my cunning as a communications officer, and it was relatively easy to find out when his ship was to be in port.

The day his ship was to arrive, I booked a flight for San Francisco and departed in the early evening. I always stayed at the little Plaza Hotel on Union Square with its ritzy El Prado restaurant when I was in the bucks and decided I needed something above the level of a fleabag. Particularly if I was just going to fling myself into a search for Fred.

From the hotel I called his ship and was told he wasn't aboard. He was on liberty. I walked straight out of the hotel, along the north side of Union Square and uphill to the Clift Hotel. The bar in the Clift was one of our favorite places to hang out. It had cozy booths and not many people went there. And there he was, sitting opposite a short and cute blond guy.

I sashayed up as though it had been planned that I would meet him there and sat down beside him. Fred looked momentarily surprised. I was introduced to the short blond. He was also on the ship and they were having an evening out in San Francisco. I wanted to strangle Fred right there in the booth, but instead gave an extremely good imitation of a very entertaining casual friend. The little blond wasn't stupid and was mystified by what was going on in front of his intelligent little eyes.

After drinks they walked me back to the Plaza Hotel, shook hands, and went back to the ship, which was tied up across the bay in Oakland.

He called the next day and we met, but it was clear he wasn't staying overnight with me at the Plaza. We didn't talk about it.

It was Russian roulette with Fred. The next time his ship came in, he called and I flew up. I took a room at the Blue Rose, a kind of collegiate pension for new arrivals in San Francisco. The Blue Rose couldn't have cared less who I had in my room, so I registered by myself. The bed was narrow in the center of a large, sunlit room. Fred seemed happy there. Neither of us complained about the bed.

His last night in San Francisco, we came out of the Clift bar into an evening so heavy with fog that it clung in Fred's curly hair in tiny droplets. He turned up the collar of the really good raincoat we'd picked out together for him. I was teaching him to dress in sport coats, gray flannel slacks, cashmere sweaters (at least one). His eyes were sapphire blue and sparkled in the streetlights, muted by the fog. He was the handsomest man in the world, there in the golden night light filtering through the dampness. We were waiting to say goodbye to some friends who were loitering in the bar. I was dumbstruck that I was about to go to a narrow bed with this blond god from the sea. Fred said, "Don't look at me like that." He made love to me very gently when we got to the Blue Rose.

The most terrible weekend of all was in a bad hotel near Union Square. It was midwinter and cold in San Francisco. When the clerk had asked me if I wanted a twin or a double bed, I requested a double. He noticed when Fred came back with me but didn't seem to care.

I had arrived to find Fred had duty the next day, so I had to kill a day by myself. I had already learned what one did when one was alone. Now I learned what one did when one was alone and waiting. The same thing: one reads. I read in that awful hotel room with its fake western furniture. Cheap wood stained a kind of orange-brown and cut to look as though it had been hacked out with an ax, like a split-rail fence. Upholstered in orange and brown plaid. Why does bad taste always seem to enjoy orange and brown and plaid? It's international.

I went down to Union Square to read on a bench, just to escape my orange-and-brown cell. I was horrified by an old woman who sat across from my bench and uncontrollably rolled her eyes and popped her false teeth out and pulled them back in. I wondered if that was what happened to you when you sat around park benches waiting for someone too long. I hurried back to the hideous hotel room. I was finding out what love was like.

The last night in that hard-mattressed dingy little room, Fred pulled me to him and said, "This is our last time, so let's make it a good one." It wasn't.

The Puzzle Box

During this time of terrible weekends in San Diego, I amused my-self by writing a short story. Called "The Puzzle Box," it was about one of those weekends and Fred's puzzling to-and-fro behavior. I, of course, veiled the homosexuality but believed for the cognoscenti the story was there. I had been very influenced by Hemingway in college and had been taught that if you revealed the arc, you revealed the cir-cle. Here's the story. I was "Peter" and Fred was "John."

THE STORY

The ship arrived at the pier exactly on time. Peter Eames decided that navy ships always did. He had gotten up at six o'clock in case the ship was early and had had to wait almost an hour for it. The guard at the gate of the navy base had refused to let him in until after eight o'clock, so he had walked along the waterfront until then.

This wasn't the first time he had met the ship, but he did exactly the same thing every time. He had hurried from the gate toward the big shed on the pier with the other civilians and stood among them on the lip of the pier now as the band played and everyone shouted.

His eyes looked anxiously along the decks, checking the face above each navy uniform. They kept returning to the superstructure. John had been up there the first time he had met the ship. That time he had been standing there as the ship nosed around the corner of the shed. Now he wasn't there. It was a very cold morning. Peter pushed his hands deeper into his overcoat pockets.

The ship was close enough for people to recognize one another, and their piercing birdlike cries were louder than the band. The band was playing a jazz tune. Military bands playing popular music always gave him chills. Suddenly John appeared at the expected place on the superstructure, looked down and waved, and went back inside. He had the radio watch that morning.

Families and friends were stationing themselves directly below their awaited ones. They did not have much to say, so they cupped their hands and shouted the same thing again and again to the smiling, uncomprehending faces above at the rail.

Peter stepped back from the edge of the pier and went back inside the freight house. He sat down beside a woman holding a child on her lap. It was chilly and damp on the bench and not quite nine o'clock yet. John probably wouldn't be able to get off the ship until noon anyway. A newsman was shouting at the foot of the gangplank. Peter went over and bought a newspaper. The newspaper had a large picture of the ship on the front and a short story. Peter had bought the same picture and story before. He went back to his bench and read the paper very carefully. When he was through, it was nine-thirty. He got up, leaving the newspaper on the bench. He put his hands in his pockets and began to stroll through the bunches of people. He walked down the pier once and on the way back noticed with a start that John was watching him from the lower deck. He went carefully over to the edge of the pier.

He smiled up and said, "Come get me."

"What?" asked John.

"I can't come aboard unless you meet me on the quarterdeck. It's cold down here. I'm coming aboard, all right?"

"Okay."

John walked away toward the quarterdeck. He was wearing his undress uniform of plain blue and his white canvas hat. He had curly blond hair, only a shade or two lighter than Peter's. He was quite a bit heavier than Peter but not fat. Peter was thin.

Peter walked over to the foot of the gangplank and explained to the marine there that he wanted to go aboard and someone would meet him. The marine said he would have to wait until that somebody appeared at the other end of the gangplank. Peter waited fifteen minutes and began to get irritable. He finally waved at someone on the quarterdeck he did not know and strode up the gangplank. An officer met him at the other end and he explained what he wanted. Just as he concluded John appeared.

He asked John with a sharp smile, "Just where in hell were you?"

John said, "What do you mean, where was I?"

"I must have waited twenty minutes down there for you. You said you'd meet me right away."

"Well, I got my mail and had to go down to the compartment. I'm sorry."

John led him up a series of ladders through a long passage and up to the radio area on the upper deck. They walked along the deck and sat down on a bench.

"How was the trip?" Peter asked.

"Same old thing." John crossed his ankles, and, tipping his hat over his eyes, slouched on the bench. He sat up again and pulled a package of Chesterfields from his sock. He gave one to Peter. He took a brown leather lighter from his jumper pocket and lit the cigarettes. Then he sat back again.

Peter sat sideways on the bench, pulling one knee up in front of him. He pulled his arms out of his coat sleeves and let the coat fall behind him. Up on the deck it was warm.

"What have you been reading?" he asked.

"I finished *Look Homeward, Angel* and I'm starting *Of Time and the River*."

They had already talked themselves out on Thomas Wolfe. They found conversation unwieldy, although John had left only a little over a month before. They always did, and neither of them were much concerned about it anymore. They knew that in a few hours they would be able to talk comfortably.

Peter asked, "Did you get my telegram?"

"Just now. I got it in the mail. Isn't it a night letter?"

"Yes."

"That's probably why they mailed it. It's very funny."

Peter said, "It's always so damned hard to send a funny telegram. You write it and it sounds great and then you have to say it slowly and carefully to the Western Union girl and you feel like a complete boob. You know, 'Yes, that's right. Dirigible. D-I-R-I-G-I-B-L-E.' And the further you go with it, the stupider it sounds. But I wanted to cheer you up a little. It really is miserable that you're not going to have a chance to get out in time to go back to school. Of course you've adjusted to the idea, but I still wanted to send it."

John was finding it hard to say something.

"Oh, it's all right. I've still got a chance if I can get transferred off the ship. I'll go over and try that while we're in port."

Peter began to tell about all the funny things that had happened to him on his trip up and during the past month. John smiled as much as he could. They were both very used to each other.

A sailor walked past them and, noticing John, asked him why he wasn't getting ready to leave the ship. He said they had announced the commencement of liberty already.

They got up and walked back down to the main deck. Peter said he would wait on the pier while John was changing his uniform. He went down the gangplank and across to the shed and sat down beside a large display of flags. It was still cold out of the sun. He got up in a few minutes and walked down to the entrance and stood in the sun. He looked at a Coca-Cola machine on the way back and noticed a small hole in the pocket of his coat. He sat down again when he got back. In a few minutes, John came down the gangplank with a group of sailors. He was carrying a small blue canvas bag. They walked slowly toward each other, smiling familiarly. It was the ship that made them awkward.

As they left the freight shed, they made for a gate directly in front of them. An old man in a guard uniform shouted at them to go through another gate and called John "Sailor."

Peter said, "I dislike bad-tempered old men. I particularly dislike bad-tempered old men who call people 'Sailor.' "

"He could have called me 'Dog,' " John said. Peter laughed and they went out the other gate.

Taxis were hard to get, and they had to share one back into town with another sailor. John sat in back with the sailor and Peter sat with the driver. They nearly struck another cab pulling away from the curb. Peter told the driver that it wasn't his fault and that people did not look where they were going when they drove. They had to go out of their way to drop off the other sailor. The cab driver had left his flag down and overcharged them. They got out and walked about three blocks to the YMCA where John kept his civilian clothes.

As they walked, Peter said, "I hate all this."

"All this what?"

"All this taking cabs with people in them and walking blocks in this section of town and then waiting for you to get out of that uniform."

"Well, it just can't be helped."

"I know it. I think that's what makes me so mad. I'm just damned mad that everything is like this."

They went in at the back door of the YMCA. John went into the locker room to change his clothes. Peter sat in a chair at one side of the ugly brown lobby and looked at the gawky boys, old women, longshoremen that passed back and forth. The lobby was decorated in shiny brown tile. Peter thought he had never seen a more hideous place. John took a long time to change.

They went out the front door and saw a cab coming far down the street. John stepped out into the street and waved it down and they climbed in. Peter gave the driver the address of his hotel. On the way to the hotel they talked over hotel room prices and decided that where Peter was staying was too expensive. They would get his luggage and check into a cheaper one.

When they arrived at the hotel, the doorman tried to take John's luggage and they had to take it out of his hands before he understood that they weren't checking in. Peter had a front room with a fire escape outside and he told John he liked that because if the hotel should burn down the people going through his room would wake him up.

They checked out and walked around the corner to a cheaper hotel. The lobby was only ten feet wide and the tile floor was broken and dirty. A mirror had been put up along one wall to widen the lobby. The desk clerk told them they could have a room for five dollars a night. The elevator was self-operating and creaky. It took a long time to get to the sixth floor. Peter told John about an apartment house in New York with the same kind of elevator. He and his sister had been trapped in it for an hour because neither of them could figure out how to open the door.

The sixth floor was soiled and hurt with its dirty white paneling and jaded wallpaper. The hall wound about several air shafts before they found their room.

The room was sordid in its attempt to look more expensive. The furniture resembled corral fences and had bright little western motifs. The rug had a meaningless design, and daylight filtered dimly from the airshaft. Peter went in to look at the bath. The tub was chipped and the towels were thin.

"I think this is about the grimmest we've hit yet," he said.

John said he thought they should go out for lunch. After lunch they went to several theaters and got tickets for that night and the following Monday night. Peter was leaving Tuesday morning, and the ship sailed Wednesday afternoon. After they bought the tickets, they went to a clothing store where John bought a pair of trousers and had a jacket altered. Peter said he was tired and wanted to take a nap before dinner, so they went back to the hotel.

When they were in bed with the shades down they both lay silently.

Suddenly Peter asked, "What's wrong?"

"Oh, you know. The same things. When you're here nothing seems wrong, but as soon as I get out to sea I begin to think things over and I get depressed. I don't really know."

Peter sat up in bed. "Damn," he said.

"Now, don't get all upset. It doesn't matter. You know that. It can't."

"Oh damn, damn, damn."

"It's really just not that important."

"You're right of course," said Peter. "It's all right. Let's get some sleep."

They got up at seven o'clock and it was eight before they were bathed and dressed. John couldn't get the bathroom window closed at the bottom and Peter stuffed a towel in the crack so the people across the court couldn't see in. Peter took the towel out when he went in to bathe. He didn't particularly care whether anyone saw in or not. The cold air that came in made him put the towel back up again. As he sat in the tub he decided to wear a suit instead of a jacket, and a black knit tie.

They hurried through dinner at a kosher delicatessen restaurant directly across the street from the theater. Peter laughed a great deal during dinner. Coming out of the restaurant, they jaywalked across to the theater. The street was dark and bright and citylike.

They saw a series of playlets and recitations by a famous theater couple. John particularly liked a Tennessee Williams bit. He was from the South. Peter often said the only minority group he really couldn't put up with was white Southerners.

When they came out of the theater, Peter was tired and wanted to go back to the hotel. John said, "Look, I'm only in port for a few days. Let's do something."

Peter didn't want to. "Like what?"

"I don't care. Let's go down to the International Settlement or someplace."

A cable car was coming up the hill. Peter ran out and jumped on it. John followed him, and they had to squeeze onto a corner of the platform and cling to a single rail. John hung half off the car. Halfway up the hill Peter changed places with him and John held him on. They were very happy and laughed all the way to end of the line. From there they walked a few blocks to a Mexican nightclub they both disliked, and left after one drink. Then they wandered down through the Italian section, peering in doors of bars they knew or had heard of. They stopped for a beer at an infamous bar because John had never been there, but didn't even stay long enough to finish their round. They finally went to a basement bar that featured classical music and paintings. They ordered beer again.

They shared their corner with a young couple who weren't talking to each other and a large picture of a sad-faced man in blue against a bright yellow background.

"Picasso-ish, do you suppose?" asked Peter.

"I don't know. Dark lines, bright color, and heavy paint is about all I make of it."

"I think he's copying van Gogh. It's too dark to see the brushwork in here, but I think that other painting over there of the two women is like van Gogh. They all seem to be by the same guy."

John settled back in his chair and studied the picture of the man in blue. The other couple in the corner stared straight ahead.

Peter went on, "I don't like it. These people that copy other artists don't have enough to them to say anything real. They think they're great and don't really understand art. You have to be great enough to have something to say before you can say it."

"I don't think you're right," John said. "They're young and have to find themselves."

"Well, of course. But we needn't think they're good just because they might be. Art is good or it isn't. Can't you see that?"

Peter didn't have as good a head as John and was getting a little drunk. When he was drunk, arguments made him angry.

"What does that picture say to you, John? Anything at all?"

John said he liked it and wouldn't be dissuaded. He actually didn't care for the picture.

About two o'clock they went back to the hotel. It was even more depressing late at night. They undressed quietly without talking and put on their pajamas.

"Thank you for bringing my pajamas," John said. Peter smiled at him and poured scotch into two glasses. He leaned against the sink with his hand under the water, waiting for it to get cold. It got hot instead so he turned it off and turned on the other tap.

"Turn off that overhead light and turn on a lamp, will you?" he asked. "This place is bad enough as it is." He ran some water into the glasses and gave one to John. "Have you a cigarette?" John lit one and gave it to him.

"Do you have duty tomorrow?" he asked John. He knew that he did.

"Yes. I tried to get a standby but I just couldn't get anyone. We're going to be in for such a short time, you know."

"It's all right. I'll get up late and do some shopping and come over after supper to the ship. You're at the supply center, aren't you?"

"Right next to it. You can come over on the train and walk to the ship. It only takes me about half an hour."

"Have you thought about going to New York when you get out?" Peter asked.

"Of course I'd like to. I don't know. If I did go, it wouldn't be because it was a challenge or was something I had to do, but only because I want to."

"It does seem impossible that we'll ever get a chance to go together. I'm going anyway. I'm not going home for more than a couple weeks myself. I'll wait until you get out and then we can travel back across the country together. I hate to think of you going back home and falling into the routine. I just can't help feeling that once I leave you there in Tennessee that you'll fall into . . . I don't know. All those people! How can you ever remember what's important with all those people saying, 'John, you're too old to go to school,' 'John, get a job,' 'John, it's time to settle down,' 'John, get a girl,' 'John, do this and that.'"

John said, "There's nothing wrong with those people. They're my family and friends and I like and want to be with them."

"I'm not trying to wean you away from them. After all, except for the navy that's all you know. But the things we've decided we want from life. Those aren't the things you can have there. You want to be a strong independent thinker and yet be a part of that kind of community. I'm telling you it can't be done. You know what they would think of me if I lived there. I'd be an eccentric. I'd be like the librarian you told me about, or the man that writes for *Harper's.* They'd all think I was funny and strange. Those are the people you'd have to depend on for intellectual companionship. Do you think you could do it?" Peter leaned back against the head of the bed and took a drink from his glass. "Oh, I suppose I'm wrong in trying to make you look at the situation like that. I'll shut up."

John stared at him with his eyes hard and bright. "Don't stop talking now!"

"Well, you know. These friends you tell me about. I'm sure they're fine, but think about them. What are they? They never do a damned thing but live graciously. That's a terrible bore if that's all you do.

What can they offer you of the things you've told me you really want?"

"What am I supposed to do?" John asked.

"How am I supposed to know what you should do? I know what I'd like you to do. 'Let's clear out together and get away from all that and find something real.' But I can't ask you to do that. I can't bear the thought of knowing you and all the things you want and seeing you become a small-town businessman. You can be greater than that!"

John said, "I know myself pretty well. I know what I want, but you just embarrass me when you say things like that."

"Damn you anyway. If I didn't believe it, I wouldn't say it! You can be great and I see you slipping away. Back into all the pressure and stupidities of that life and I can't do a thing about it. Not one single thing." He stopped and stared down at the glass in his hands.

"Now you're making me mad," John said. "And that's what you want to do I suppose. You use the shock treatment on me to get me thinking. I could do it to you too, you know."

"I know you could."

They talked on for several hours and went to sleep at nearly five o'clock.

At six o'clock the alarm went off and Peter leaped from bed. He woke John and got his uniform from the closet. John sleepily got into various pieces as he was handed them. Peter dropped his hat on his head, opened the door, and shoved him out of it gently. "I'll come over just before six o'clock," he said. "I'll eat dinner before I come."

Peter got back in bed and slept until noon. He woke up and looked around the room. The barren room in the daylight was so tawdry that he jumped out of bed hurriedly and went into the bathroom. By one o'clock he had bathed and dressed and was eating breakfast.

He spent the afternoon buying Christmas presents and arranging for their mailing. He finished about three o'clock. Seeing a book he wanted to read on the stands, he decided to go read in the square.

He settled down on a cold bench among the old men and the pigeons and started reading. It was a book John had written him about. His reading was interrupted by an old woman on another bench who was making spitting and blubbering noises with her mouth and pushing them back in with her fists. No one else paid any attention to her. The woman next to her was ponderous and made up like a clown. After a while she looked at the blubberer and said, "What do you think you are, a motorboat?" Peter was sickened by it and was suddenly overcome by the decrepit and ruined people surrounding him. He pulled his coat tighter and lit a cigarette. The sun had fallen behind the buildings and it was cold and sad in his corner of the square. He wanted very much to leave but it wasn't time to eat yet and he was sure the hotel room would be even sadder than the square. The woman stopped blubbering and very matter-of-factly put some false teeth in her mouth. Peter wondered if she was mad or was doing a gum-strengthening exercise. He didn't care enough to think about it long.

The square was nearly empty when he finished the book and went back to the hotel room. He stopped only long enough to change his shirt and tie and wash his hands. He looked in the mirror before leaving and decided that he didn't much care for his looks.

He had a quick supper and caught the five-thirty train across the bay. It was dark when the train left him at the supply center. The ship's mast and superstructure jutted from behind a large freight shed and he walked in that direction. As he walked along the pier he had to move aside to avoid some workmen off-loading cargo.

The gangplank was brightly lighted and the officer of the deck stood stiffly at the top like a dummy in a store window. It wasn't the same officer that had been there when the ship first pulled in. He had a sailor go look for John, and Peter stared at lists on a bulletin board until he came down.

They climbed the gray painted ladders again and went into the radio shack. They had only started to talk when another radioman came in. John introduced him and they left him on watch and went to a lounge across the passage. John was called away immediately to the telephone. When he came back, he had a roll of Japanese prints and a wooden box.

They looked at the prints and John pointed out the one he wanted Peter to keep for him. The others could be given to their friends. Peter liked several of them, especially a black-and-white figure of a geisha.

John's favorite was a gray-and-purple print of a Japanese street at sunset. John was called away again and as he left he said, "See if you can get that puzzle box open by the time I get back."

Peter picked up the box from the table. It was covered with intricate designs and was apparently a solid oblong block. Both the top and the bottom had a painted design. He started pulling and tugging at it.

When John came back about half an hour later, Peter had his head bent over the box and was still pulling and tugging at it. He looked up at John and said, "You've just got to remember me and what I said, that's all."

John sat down across the green-covered table and lit a cigarette. He looked thoughtful and said, "I'll try."

Shortly after nine John was called away again, and when he hadn't returned by a quarter to ten Peter put on his coat and picked up the pictures and wooden box. He went across to the radio room and told the radioman there to tell John he had left.

He thought John was probably talking to another ship on the telephone at the quarterdeck, and he'd just say good-bye. John wasn't there. The officer of the deck looked at Peter curiously but didn't say anything as he left.

The pier was dark and vastly empty, the isolated lights only making it emptier. It wasn't late, but no one was to be seen on the walk back to the train stop. There was something lifelike about the tracks. They seemed to breathe softly in the quiet night. Peter couldn't find where the train stopped and finally had to ask a man sitting in a watchman's shanty. When it came, the train was bleak and bright inside and the black night seemed to be pressing to get in at the few passengers.

Peter slept late again the next day and, not wanting to stay in the room or sit in the square, he spent the early part of the afternoon in the stores. John was supposed to come at four o'clock. At three Peter went back to the room with a newspaper. He sat in an uncomfortable chair and put his feet up on the desk and read the paper. When he finished the paper, he read a book he had bought for John's Christmas present. Then he filed his fingernails. He was shaving when John arrived at five o'clock.

"What time do you leave tomorrow?" Peter asked.

"Sometime in the afternoon."

"I'll catch the limousine out to the airport at quarter to seven. I don't have to go that early, but there's no point in my staying to see the ship, is there?"

"No, I wouldn't like that particularly," John said.

They went to an expensive restaurant for dinner and drank *vin rosé*. John talked about his father's business and Peter listened intently. He liked to hear John talk. Toward the end of dinner a large party of businesspeople came in and sat near them. They all laughed and talked in a nervous manner and did not seem to know one another very well. They told dirty stories in loud voices.

After John and Peter left the restaurant, they stopped at India House for a drink they liked, Pimm's Cups. Peter told a story he had told several times about a party he had gone to on Telegraph Hill that had started at that very bar. It was a funny story and the ending was not true, but John knew that.

When they went up to the corner to catch a taxi, they couldn't find one. Two middle-aged women across the street were looking for one too. A cab finally came down their side of the street and they motioned to the women to take it, but just then another cab came up.

The play that night was old-fashioned and so was the star. Neither of them enjoyed it very much and when it was through they went directly back to the hotel. They each had a scotch and water and a cigarette and sat back in the hard chairs with their feet up. The overhead light was on.

They sat silently for awhile. Peter finally said, "I hate going back tomorrow."

"So do I, but it won't be so long. I'll be back in a little over a month."

"It will really go quite fast, I suppose."

"Be sure and give Phil some of those pictures. But don't give him that one that I like the best."

"I will," Peter said. "And you, you'll try to remember me and what we've been talking about?"

"Of course. But you know how I feel about this. That it's wrong for you to shut yourself away and not let new people and things come into your life."

"I know myself. I'm Peter Eames and if I go on as I always used to, I'll not only forget what's important for myself, but I'll forget what's so important about you and for you. And if I forget, I'm afraid you'll forget too."

"I will try to remember."

They stayed awake very late and had to hurry the following morning. As Peter was packing, John said, "I never get over how much stuff you can get in a suitcase."

Peter was wedging the rolled-up pictures and the puzzle box into his suitcase. The pictures fit along the front. He pulled out a pair of shoes and put the box in their place. It didn't fit. He pulled out a stack of soiled underwear. The box went in neatly but he couldn't get the clothing back in. Finally he took the box out and looked at it carefully. It was battered and a little worn. John met his glance. He bent over the suitcase again and firmly pushed the shoes in one direction and underwear in the other. Forcing the puzzle box between them, he pressed the lid down on the suitcase and latched it.

John was waiting at the door. He looked young and drowsy.

Peter picked up his suitcase and his raincoat and took one last look around the room.

"Let's go," he said.

Morning was just graying the streets and it was cold when they left the hotel. The Yellow Cab that pulled up at the curb looked warm and friendly. They went to the YMCA first so John could check his civilian clothes back in. Peter waited in the cab and was unhappy.

John reappeared in a few minutes and they drove off through the silent city streets. Peter got out at the airline ticket agency. "I'll see you in about a month," he said to John. John looked dim and shadowy in the cab's interior. "Good-bye," he said.

Peter watched the cab go down the street, but John didn't look back. He knew he wouldn't. He picked up his suitcase and turned toward the curb. Carefully he thought about nothing.

Letters to My Mother

Rereading my letters to my mother from this period is disconcerting. I was so slick. So verbal. I guess everything you could expect from an English major who was concealing his homosexuality from his mother as well as everyone else. It was as though there were two channels going at the same time. I guess I thought the homosexual one would go away someday, like so many homosexuals did and do.

I had had something like a nervous breakdown aboard the aircraft carrier. That, too, I concealed pretty much. Its effect lingered on for months and I was afraid it would return. Fred brought an end to all that. Even so, in my letters there are flashes. These are some of the things I wrote my mother:

January, U.S. Naval Training Station, Newport, Rhode Island

> There are three of us with birthdays within four days so tomorrow night we're going to take a large rowdy group into Newport and have a party. Now I'll be twenty-two and I have to shape up I guess. You still get away with a lot of things at twenty-one that you just feel too old to do at twenty-two.

I signed my letters "Bill" at this time. After Fred I notice I began signing both "Bill" and "William" and eventually only "William."

5 April, The Hotel Whitcomb, San Francisco

> One of the greatest things about flying at night is seeing cities from the air. Chicago looks like a million acres of carnival and Denver looked like an emerald tiara. It is built on a mountainside I guess and has the shape of a crescent and the lights looked mostly green for some reason.

This cross-country trip to join a ship in the Pacific was my second flight. The plane had to land to refuel in Chicago, St. Louis, Denver, and Salt Lake City before landing in San Francisco.

29 April, USS *Adirondack*

As you can see I finally caught up with the old girl today, over here in Alameda, which is across the bay from San Francisco and a little south of Oakland. Strangely enough I was as cool as a cucumber coming aboard and since I refused to let myself think about it prior to its happening no mental agonies or nervousness occurred.

Can't really tell you much about the ship except it may be a baby carrier but it's a big baby!

I in fact almost fainted before forcing myself down the pier and aboard the huge ship.

8 September, USS *Adirondack*

My first watch on the bridge as Junior Officer of the Deck was Saturday. We ran into a squall and as the clouds approached the sea turned lilac, shading to amethyst and deep purple directly around the ship—and the sky—there is just so much sky!

Sky stretches in every direction and contains every kind of cloud imaginable, all at once. Long streaky clouds, big bumpy clouds, lacy filigree, all in great profusion capping an endless expanse of water it seems, yet it is only fifteen miles to the horizon.

There is just too much of everything. Last night the moon was scudding through the clouds and bare patches of star-studded sky glistened through the rents in the soft blanket of cloud banks also. For one brought up on the Currier and Ives delights of Lake Michigan it's just too much of a bundle at one time.

24 September, USS *Adirondack*

The sunsets here in the China Sea are astounding. Almost useless to try to describe but a careless hand piles huge black thunderheads against a gray and gold sky that turns to brass. The new moon clambers out of the inky sky and holding baby stars by the hand, wanders through drifting mists of cloud and on up into a heaven complete with every star that could possibly be visible.

23 December, USS *Adirondack*

Mother, just briefly I'll tell you that I've been going through quite an emotional and mental hell the last few months, finding out things about myself, making up my mind about what I must believe and what I must do. I know it's not over, perhaps will never be; but today I feel much stronger and more content than I have in many months. I sometimes wonder if perhaps your sister Madge was struggling through the same sort of things and simply made her mind up in a different direction.

My mother's much older sister had committed suicide inexplicably when my mother was still very young.

This is the only indication in my letters in any kind of direct way that I was in emotional trouble. The tone is quite different from the glibness of most of my letters.

5 January, aboard the aircraft carrier the USS *Adirondack*

> Another day, another typhoon. One bearing down and another dead ahead. I just came down from the bridge, a black pitching void around all sides, an occasional comber breaking across the forward end of the flight deck, the deck beneath your feet swooping down, then bucking several times, shivering back up, tilting one way and the other, and swooping down again. Quite exhilarating and I feel most savage and unrestrained with the wind whistling through the struts of the planes and the banging of loose hatches and the creaking of deck plates. Then a match illuminates the face of the phone talker who is braced against the side of the deck house, holding his phones on his head and lighting a cigarette and very bored.

13 February, Friday the 13th, USS *Adirondack*

> On coming back from the shower this evening I opened my cabinet door and noticed a sprig of evergreen and berry I had taped there some time ago. I poked my nose into it and breathed deeply the smell of my unsensational, dearly beloved western Illinois. It reminded me of the banks of tiger lilies moistly pungent in the hot summer sun; banked against the warmly red woodshed and the three stepping stones Dad put down through the gap in the hedge and putting the dishcloths out to dry on the sunny bank in the side yard. It reminded me of tall evergreen heaped with fluffy snow on every limb, which moist little tongues would lick, and then ice-beaded mittens would pull down and let fly and red fat faces would turn up to a miniature snowfall.
>
> It reminded me of my blue knitted cap with a V shape that came down over the forehead and two more over each ear that I always put on backwards, it reminded me of snow angels, it reminded me of a funeral for a crushed celluloid doll in the side yard with doll friends present in their chairs while Aunt Dore Hinman stood across her cinder-graveled drive next door and laughed.

I also write very seriously about God in the letters of this period. As my mother was relatively religious, she probably accepted this as the inevitable result of spending so much time at sea, although she would

not have liked too much fervency. As my father and two older brothers had been in the navy, she was certainly used to letters from sailors
as well as communicating with God. I must have prayed a lot that I
wouldn't succumb to my nervous condition, which I was concealing
from everyone.

In one letter I wrote,

> Did I ever tell you that the enlisted men in my communication division on
> the ship called me 'The Sweetheart of Café Society'?

This note surprised me. I have no memory of this, but evidently the
enlisted men were rather proud of their flighty young blond officer
who partied a great deal and left the ship wearing Brooks Brothers
clothes. My image had been smoothed up a lot since I had come to the
West Coast. My fellow officers from better schools and better backgrounds were teaching me a lot. And I was a quick student.

My letters are peppered with frequent references to lying in the sun
to get a tan. I was very conscious of being thin and hoped to improve
the overall look with being brown. It is almost heartbreaking to read
of my efforts to gain weight above my normal 160 pounds. At one
point I approached 170 and was thrilled. Now it seems like a fantasy.

I also frequently discuss plans to come home on leave, which never
happened as my ship was rarely in port for more than three or four
days and the policy was that no officers could miss a trip. I finally
wound up crossing the Pacific fourteen times.

28 August, USS *Adirondack*

> One of the loveliest things I have ever seen is the fishing fleet leaving
> San Diego channel just before dawn. We were coming in and a light mist
> hung over the channel. Dawn was breathing down our necks but not too
> heavily. As I looked down from the height of the ship's bridge a fleet of
> small white fishing boats glided noiselessly by on the dark waters, each
> bearing a small white light. It seemed to me as though they were nuns,
> each bearing a votive candle and gliding down some dark and polished
> cathedral aisle, not a sound or disturbance as they set to work in the most
> beautiful part of the day. As I turned to look after them the moon hung

over a bank of blue clouds and looked like a cantaloupe ball, orange and juicy.

2 February, Treasure Island, Bachelor Officers' Quarters, San Francisco

My new address is:

USNS *Henrietta Peabody*
c/o Fleet Post Office
San Francisco, Calif.

Now it seems that we were going to Eniwetok, which is very close to Bikini, as is Kwajalein, all three taking part in the test. I think I'll be gone for a shorter time than I anticipated as the ship's orders read that she is to be back here April 28.

In other letters from the *Peabody* I write about my plans for entering the diplomatic corps and also about the short stories I am writing and submitting to magazines.

2 April, Bikini, Marshall Islands

One unusual thing about the bombs is their glorious colors. I've never seen a film of them in color, but they have the brightest oranges and yellows imaginable and shade into the most beautiful violet and mauve. The underside of the cloud is edged with bright pink and as the cloud grows the colors gradually shift and change also. Extremely beautiful for the enormous power it contains.

In addition to the letters I sent to my mother, I edited a ship newspaper. It was extremely tongue-in-cheek, collegiate, and fatuous. But it did contain an amusing advertising section that simply asked, "Men, Have You Tried Beer?"

My Nervous Breakdown

I didn't have a nervous breakdown when I was with Fred but I had had something very close to it aboard the aircraft carrier the previous fall. On my first trip out on the *Adirondack,* we made a long crossing to Japan. We went to the port of Yokosuka. The port town was tacky, with little nightclubs full of evening-gowned hostesses and small hotels/whorehouses. Over the main street of bars some wit had given a slogan to an enterprising advertiser, who had draped a large banner from one side of the street to the other. It read DRINK SUNTORY WHISKEY. IT GIVES YOU A HEADACHE.

Some other junior officers and I took a train to Tokyo and there, too, it was all wet, black streets, neon lights, a sea of black umbrellas above which we tall Americans loomed. One morning we visited the Imperial Palace. On a green embankment overlooking the moat an impossibly tiny child was seated alone wearing a flat straw boater hat. He had a sketch pad on his knee and was painting a very accomplished watercolor of the palace. He looked about two. I was impressed.

One day we bought train tickets at random, having no idea where we were going. We did that often on later trips. In the spring, just before I left the ship to go to Bikini, we were in a small provincial town sitting on a balcony of a little hotel. "We" were my best friends from the ship, Ken, who was my roommate, and John David. Ken was married and John David and I both tried to avoid the subject of why we never went to whorehouses.

From this balcony perch we saw a very drunken man slipping and sliding down the muddy street below, a large branch of cherry blossoms on his shoulders. Drunkenness on the streets was common for sailors. Very uncommon for the Japanese. Housewives peered out of their doorways and small children followed him laughing and pointing. There was much of that tittering behind your hand that the Japanese favor. He was big for a Japanese man, our drunk, and was singing a song, probably welcoming spring. He lost his footing and fell against a wall into the mud. He lay there for a bit, face to the wall, under his cherry blossoms, still singing merrily. After a time he heaved himself to his feet and wandered off, trailing urchins behind him. I have always remembered him, the man who fell in the mud singing beneath his blossoms.

After that first trip to Japan we had been detailed to continue to Hong Kong under great secrecy. There we picked up the remains of the Flying Tiger air fleet. General Claire Chennault had owned this private airline under Chiang Kai-shek and it had been seized by the Communists. How it wound up in a court case in Hong Kong is anybody's guess, but the English had surprisingly awarded the planes to Chennault and we had been sent in to get them. They were blackened wrecks, but we hauled them aboard and set off at top speed for Long Beach, California, to deliver them. In Long Beach we looked over the rail to watch the still sprightly, gray-haired and hatchet-faced Chennault on the pier greeting our arrival. He was with his much younger and beautiful Chinese wife.

As soon as I could get off the ship I rushed about buying things I somehow felt I had to have. Painting supplies so I could have something to do besides read in those wastes of empty time aboard ship. And many other odds and ends I felt I *had* to get immediately.

Back aboard ship at the dinner table, I suddenly felt an overwhelming compulsion to scream. I excused myself and went rapidly to the communication center on an upper deck immediately below the bridge. I had become an expert communication officer during the trip and my best moments were in the darkened center with its green glowing radar screens and quick-witted enlisted men. Geary was there on duty, the only black on the communication crew.

Geary wasn't a kid. He was a solidly built mature man. There was something reassuring in his presence. After chatting aimlessly a bit, I moved on. I felt as long as I was moving I wouldn't scream. I went to the fantail, walked across the flight deck. I went to the hangar deck where they were showing *Lost in Alaska* with Abbott and Costello. I couldn't sit through papier-mâché igloos and the Ivory Snow falling snowflakes. I finally wound up in my cabin three decks down, well below the water line. The fact that we were tied up in port made it worse. The real world was right there, just at the end of the hawser lines and I was trapped in this enormous metal labyrinth.

Ken was ashore. His family was in San Diego, which wasn't far away. His beautiful blonde wife had come to the pier and spirited him away. I might have confided in him but I doubt it.

I lay in my bunk with the lights out and the horrible feeling that I was about to scream swept over me, stronger and stronger. I sat up and turned on the light. Among my books was a copy of the complete works of Shakespeare that I'd had in college. Beaten up and blue. I'd carried it aboard ship thinking finally I would have time to read it. I started reading. As long as my eyes were consuming words I wouldn't scream. I had no idea what I was reading, but line by line I forged forward. I read all night long, hanging on second by second, line by line.

During the day things were a little better. Ensign Gordon across the passage was aboard. His presence in the bathroom consoled me a bit. He was like a shaggy retriever, head down and wagging a bit as he grinned and wanted to be liked. You could feel his missing tail waving back and forth.

Routine carried me through the day. I had to be here and there, in the officer's mess, the communication center. I felt like a big puppet being put through its paces. I smiled. I talked. I wasn't there.

We sailed that night for San Diego, having unloaded all of General Chennault's planes. The movement didn't help much. I read Shakespeare all that night, too. Ken was in the bunk below me but didn't seem to notice that I was up with my light on all night.

I must have fallen asleep here and there, but the hanging on went on for weeks. After Shakespeare I shifted to the Bible. In my letters to my mother I state that I am going through a period of great stress but I don't elaborate. Lying in bed with the fear of screaming haunting me, I devised a method of closing my mind. I pretended that my head was a four-sided pergola on top of the house of my body. There were four windows; one on each side, each equipped with a white pull-down shade. As an idea attempted to enter my mind by a window, I would pull down the shade. And as the thought would try to enter each window successively, in turn the shades came down, leaving my mind a white, empty cube. A shade would roll up, a thought would try to enter, and I would quickly pull the shade down again. If the white empty space could remain empty long enough, I could sleep.

I must have prayed a lot, too. In rereading my letters home, I find many references to God and how I had been able to count on him. I have no memory of this having been the case, but certainly every stratagem I could manage I called into play so as not to lose control of myself. I didn't know exactly what would happen to a junior officer who became hysterical aboard ship, but I knew it couldn't be good.

And I had the example of Ensign Posey before me—Mr. Posey, who had been taken to sick bay and no more was seen or heard of him.

Rigidly I somehow maintained my composure. Smiled and walked through the paces of being all right. Saw friends in San Francisco when we sailed there before departing again for the Orient. It was like a delicate tightrope walk. I could go for some hours feeling relatively normal, and suddenly there would be that roller-coaster swoop and I would feel on the brink of losing control.

We were back in San Francisco by Christmas, where I had duty on Christmas Eve. Ken smuggled cocktails aboard in his youngest child's baby bottle, along with his family. There were always these little flickers of conviviality and warmth here and there in our lives aboard the gray metal behemoth, but always the ship loomed large about me like some brooding, threatening floating castle from which I would be lucky to emerge alive. There was talk of sending me to cryptographic school in Monterey in the spring.

During the major typhoons we encountered off Japan in mid-winter I was better. Every moment was taken with holding onto something. On the wildly swaying bridge, whipping back and forth in the black void, the wind howling, hanging many feet directly above the black waves as the ship rolled to one side, then looking straight down over the flight deck to the water below it as it rolled to the other, I was exhilarated. There was a very real danger that the carrier would capsize. This smaller type, built on a merchant ship hull, had been known to roll over in severe storms. But it did not seem dangerous, just enormously thrilling as huge waves broke over the bow and ran back over the flight deck and crashed into the pit of the elevator opening. The giant elevators were kept down in bad weather to reduce the rolling. Even going to my cabin below the waterline didn't disturb me. I was distracted and it was an enormous relief.

The hanging on minute by minute went on for perhaps four or five months. I confided in no one. I spent days on end without sleeping to any degree. I became expert at insulating my brain in its empty little white cupola. Many years later a friend who had studied comparative religion, when I told him about this experience, said, "But that's what the Buddhists do. They empty their minds. You were emptying your mind."

Whether it was the emptying or the praying I don't know, but finally one night as I lay there with my Shakespeare propped up on my chest, it came to me: "Either you will have the strength to survive this constant need to scream and go crazy, or you will not. It is like a mathematical formula. You must try to have the strength to survive it, but if you do not have enough strength you will not survive it." This thought calmed me. And though the struggle went on, the panic within me subsided.

When I finally escaped to study cryptography in Monterey I was in much better shape. But I felt as though I was a glass window in its frame that had been shattered but had not fallen apart. All the pieces were there, in place but forever broken. They would never be whole again. I would never be thoughtless and insensitive again. I had to be careful. Even when I lay down upon my bed in the cavernous rooms of the officers' quarters in what had been the very grand Monterey Peninsula Hotel, built by the Dole pineapple fortune, I was cautious. At any moment I was ready for those hysterical feelings to sweep over me. During the four months I was at this school, I began to feel scar tissue form, binding the shards together. And it was this scarred person that Fred had met aboard the ship bound for Bikini. A person who seemed confident and knowledgeable but was still emotionally convalescent. And who desperately needed Fred's large, strong arms around him to ward off the unknown threats, the dangers that lurked.

Fred's Clothes

In my letters to my mother I talk about my clothes a lot. Civilian clothes. I had discovered Brooks Brothers in San Francisco and was learning a good deal about the right clothes from my fellow junior officers. Or at least where to get them.

Brooks Brothers was on a second floor—could it have been on Post Street, near Union Square? It was all obviously correct. The tweed jackets, the rep ties, the button-down collars. I bought a gray tweed herringbone jacket, flat front dark gray flannel pants, a tie or two. Cordovan shoes in a dark mahogany were de rigueur to wear with such an ensemble. With my height and blond hair I actually looked quite Ivy League and would have been the last one to deny it.

Subsequently I wrote home to explain why I needed a dark blue linen suit, a tan summer wool suit, a blazer. Much later Fred wrote to me when I had gotten a sizable raise in a new job in New York: "Now you should just about be earning what you're spending."

Why I felt I needed to justify to my mother the spending of money on civilian clothes I have no idea. I had worked my way through college and had managed a wardrobe that had included a tuxedo even then.

Fred had virtually no civilian clothes. I began to provide them for him. And he bought some of them for himself. Soon he was wearing gray flannel pants. Button-down broadcloth shirts. A white one and blue one. Fred had no problem in being taught how to dress. He liked his new clothes. He looked handsome in them. And when we were both in civilian clothes, the differences in rank were erased. I was two years older than Fred but it wasn't evident. Running around San Francisco, we were just two tall blond guys wearing upper-middle-class clothing no one could quibble about.

When we were visiting in Monterey, the new duds were admired by my sister-in-law Marie's father, who was also visiting. "Where did you get that jacket?" he asked. "I'd like to get one like it." I was flattered, as he had been many years abroad in American consular work and was what I considered to be a sophisticated man of the world. "You probably couldn't afford it," Marie said.

For our first Christmas after leaving Bikini, I got Fred a maroon cashmere V-necked sweater. It cost seventy dollars. That was a lot of money. I wonder if I earned that much a week. I had one in navy blue. Maroon was a tiny bit flashier than navy blue or camel hair, the staple colors. He was knocked out. I got him maroon socks to match.

In whatever fatigued hotel or rooming house in which we were staying, I polished his cordovan shoes while he napped so he would be resplendent in maroon sweater, socks, and shoes when we stepped out on Christmas day. He opened his eyes from the bed to look at me seated on the floor with shoe shine rag and polish in hand. "You don't have to polish my shoes," he said. "I want to polish your shoes," I said.

Fred was very sexy in his bell-bottom work dungarees and unironed blue navy-issue shirt. He was sexy too in his dark blue dress uniform. The navy uniform made the most out of a man's muscles. But in his well-tailored Brooks Brothers clothes he had a very different image. Without his white navy cap pushed back on his tight blond curls he looked more mature, more reserved. Fred had a wonderful grin and in his uniform he was very cute. In his civilian clothes he became handsome. Particularly when a tan raincoat, Burberry style, was added to his wardrobe. Why should a man's clothes make me love him more? But Fred's did.

Or perhaps it was as though Fred was my big doll to dress up and play with. The more dressed up he was, the more he was mine.

I Waited in San Francisco

I was discharged in San Diego a month before Fred was let out of the navy in San Francisco. It was March when I arrived. I rented a studio apartment with a Murphy bed in a relatively nice building for one month. It had a very large mirror on one wall that swiveled around and revealed a double bed on its backside that let down. Once down it fairly well filled the room. It wasn't hideously furnished, that studio. It had a bay window with a pretty, plump settee in it, a nice carpet, tables and chairs. All kind of 1930s but not poor 1930s.

Fred's ship was in port much of the time I was waiting it out in that little apartment, always filled with that gray light that is the curse of San Francisco. No ho-hum, this is spring, to be followed by summer, to be followed by autumn. Every day is much like every other day, whole seasons rolling regularly around every twenty-four hours. You must *do* something, you must *feel* something. San Francisco doesn't let you slip into brain-dead routine. It's hard.

We were having a warm March, that spring of 1955. The apartment had access to the roof, and I went there to sunbathe in those long afternoons waiting for Fred to arrive. The ship was undergoing repairs and he was able to leave most evenings. But that left me the entire day to fill in one way or another.

Being tan was a fetish in those years. Not only with me. Because of my thinness I fancied that my body looked better tan. But so did many other people. It was the Palm Beach look, suggesting that you had the time to loll about swimming pools.

Lying there one afternoon, I suddenly recalled a dream that I had had the night before in that fold-down bed. I had been walking across a kind of Arcadian landscape as the sun set. One of those Poussin-like places where you expect to see nymphs dancing and satyrs chasing them. Corot did a lot of those kinds of scenes, too. But in all fairness to myself, I hadn't seen any of those yet.

On a hill I saw one of those little decorative temples they used to build as garden follies in the eighteenth century. I hadn't ever seen one of those yet either.

With my eyes shut against the sun I was very much aware of the hot gravel roof on which I was lying and the smell of the tar that underlay the gravel. It was a hard surface to lie on. And behind my eyelids in the darkness I could clearly see that little temple. The setting sun fell clearly on the word "Love" on the band of stone that ran under the small dome. And in the shadow that fell on the right side of the temple I could see another word. It said "Death." Between them, cut on an angle, was a curly little "and." I felt frightened. Or did in the dream.

In later years when I felt fright in a dream that wasn't essentially frightening, I came to interpret it to mean I should remember the moment. It was a kind of emotional exclamation point. I didn't understand that then. Or perhaps I did.

I mulled it over and considered that perhaps love and death were the same thing. That the sense of being all right, of being safe, of being warm and secure that I felt with Fred was just a harbinger of things to come. That we came from somewhere in which love surrounded us all the time. And that we searched to re-create those feelings here. And eventually we would go back there.

I went downstairs and wrote a relatively awful poem of twelve stanzas, four lines each, which I titled "Greek Revival." I read it to Fred when he arrived from the ship that evening. He wasn't bowled over.

I have quite a lot of poetry from that last period when I was stationed in San Diego. Probably because I had a lot of time on my hands. Probably because, being an incurable romantic, I felt that romantic people did that. Captured their emotions in poems. I had never written poetry in college. In fact, I thought that people who did were awfully dim or wet or whatever term we used for students who weren't hard and fast and witty. Which was very much the style of those hard-drinking years when I was in college with the veterans of World War II who were all five to ten years older than I was.

Now I was just as wet and dim as the Bruces and Evelyns I thought so poorly of a few years earlier.

The bulk of my poetry had to do with my inability to convince Fred that loving me was important. Fred clearly saw it as a phase that he was going through and the sooner he stopped sleeping with me the sooner he would be able to forget that it ever happened. And yet. And yet.

He had lain in the sun with me on the roof on a Sunday afternoon when he had liberty and when we came back down to my apartment had stripped off his trunks, climbed on top of me, and inserted himself in my body. This was unusual. We hadn't done it again since that drunken afternoon when I had cried so much on being told that he wasn't going to sleep with me anymore.

This was real fucking. After he pulled out, it was his turn to cry. He put on my cotton bathrobe and curled up on the little puffed-up settee and sobbed, crying "Mother, Mother" between his sobs. I didn't feel sorry for him. Or perhaps I deeply resented being placed in the role of the tempter urging him to sin. At any rate, I felt only scorn for his sobbing bulk over on the too-small settee.

Despite these flurries of hatred for me, we continued to make plans for our futures. Fred's brother was coming to San Francisco with his girlfriend Muriel from Bozeman. Fred and I were going to buy his car from him after driving back to Bozeman and continue on to Fred's home in Kansas. I would fly home ahead of him, he would come through my hometown and pick me up, and we would go to New York together.

I had made major plans to enter the diplomatic corps. My letters home were full of it. I had taken the tests for entry in San Francisco with little preparation and had come close to passing. But now I had lost interest. Simultaneously with falling ever more in love with Fred, I had been planning a career that would carry me far away from him. The reality of being in love with him, the realization that the diplomatic corps wasn't going to be that much different from the navy, the amazing fact that Fred actually had a job waiting for him in New York, led me to shelve any ideas about doing anything other than going to New York and trying my luck there.

Fred's father had friends on Wall Street and had wangled a summer apprenticeship there for his son. Even though Fred cried out for his mother after fucking me proper, he made an effort to go to New York with me after his discharge from the navy. This was not lost on me. I gave myself over to my fate.

Three Poems

When Fred and I were really so much in love with each other in that terrible rooming house in San Francisco, we were moved to write poems. Poems just as terrible as the room.

Love is like having a baby or surviving a typhoon. You remember that it was like some kind of religious revelation. Or maybe taking drugs. And you write it down. Later when you've sobered up, the words don't capture the experience at all. It was beyond those words, the experience. But there you have it. The words are all that's left. These were the poems I wrote.

YOU SAID, "TOO SOON TO START, TOO LATE TO STOP."

You said, "Too soon to start, too late to stop."
And jarred my life and heart awake.
My life so well ordered and,
If not complete, controlled
Into a vague reality.

Controlled, complete, are these words for the
Living?
Rather words for those who die.
There is no plan for love,
No time or place for its singularity.
You have taught me that.

I know the desperate calmness life can be,
And I can face that again
For I have known what loving is and
I echo in my heart your words,
"Thank God, it was too late to stop."

You Said, "Your Body Is Very Warm."

You said, "Your body is very warm."
As you held me against your great
Warm and golden body,
Golden with warmth and golden with love,
And it was started.

For my blood is that New England blood,
Slow to warm and quick to doubt.
Unused to sentiment and love.
Used only to myself
And coolness.

You held me against your
Warm and golden heart. I think
There is a cold hysteria in ice
Compared to which the frailest
Flame has strength.

You Said, "We Must Try To Remember This."

And when I enter this lonely room
The memory of you sweeps over me
And grips me so tightly I gasp.
And you said, "We must try to remember this."

Obviously I had been very influenced by Edna St. Vincent Millay in my college literary courses. I think I wanted to *be* Edna St. Vincent Millay. All full of fire and the pure urge to live life to the fullest. And never a million laughs.

I'm sure I was fulfilling those urges in my romance with Fred. There's always that horrible feeling when you're in your twenties that you're going to be left out. But there was more to it than that with Fred. There was more to it than that.

Some Men Who Slept with Other Men, No. 2*

I SLEPT WITH ABRAHAM LINCOLN

Abraham Lincoln was very sexual. When he was in love with me, we engaged in sexual activity at least daily. Frequently more often. My heart used to go out to him when he was married to that short, fat woman. She was so fussy she couldn't have been much comfort to him in bed. One of those "lie there and get it over with" kind of women. Of that I'm sure.

We shared a room when we were both young men in Springfield. Above the law offices where we worked. And a bed. He was tall and gave the appearance of being gangly. But he was graceful actually. And had a lot of muscles. All that rail splitting made him sinewy. He had the appearance of being a real frontier person. You wouldn't have been surprised to see him in deerskin pants and a coonskin cap. But only his face and hands were weathered. The skin of his body was very white and fine.

I knew him well for only a few years, but I knew him very well during that time. There was always something wistful about him. As though he needed more love than he got. His mother died when he was young, you know, and although he had a stepmother who cared for him and encouraged him, it wasn't the same. It can't be.

I was much more sexually advanced than he was when we met. I never asked him, but I think he was a virgin or as good as. I, on the other hand, had been brought up as a town boy and had always had a pretty body that other boys enjoyed. It was commonplace then. Beds were shared. Bodies were shared. If you were caught, parents would

---

*Another story I wrote for Fred. He never commented.

108

admonish you. But it didn't matter very much. We were on the frontier. Illinois was nothing but woods and clearings. Even in town there was a lot of work to do. Water had to be carried, gardens weeded, animals fed, horses curried, stables cleaned. We were surviving, and not badly. Men and women had sex to procreate and create a family who could help them with their labors. Lucky was the farm family that had ten children. Owning lots of land and making some money was a real possibility for them. But sex as an amusement was far from their minds. As was love.

But, as I said, I had been brought up in a town. My mother had been a teacher, so we had books in the house. I read Wordsworth and Shelley. No Lord Byron, that would have been too shocking. But poems about love and being one with nature. All those kinds of things.

Emerson and Thoreau and the New England writers I liked less. That's where one's own temperament played a part. I was an emotional person. Being self-reliant and hewing my own moral way was not of great interest. Of course we didn't even know Emily Dickinson existed. I would have liked her poetry very much. Abraham would have, too. He was very romantic—he just never got a chance to express it very much.

Not to say that he wasn't ambitious. He was that. But he wasn't narrow minded or money minded. I think, coming from the kind of dirt-poor family that he did, it came as quite a surprise to him that he was smart and could do just as well as anyone else.

His love for me, which was intense, would not have stood in the way of his continuing to rise. I don't think he dreamed of being president when I knew him, but he certainly dreamed of being well known. Of living in a decent house. Of being married to someone of a much better background than his own.

With me, it was the first time that he hadn't been really alone. We would go to bed at night and he would tell me what he hoped to do, what he planned to do, and I would tell him that it was all possible. He liked being held in my arms. There was a babyish side to him. But when he was aroused his passions swept him into being very dominating and very male. He liked to kiss and he was a good kisser. He had a very fresh-tasting mouth. He didn't chew tobacco or drink.

But at a certain point his passions would rise and he would push me onto my stomach and apply himself. He had big hands and feet so he was large in that department, too, but he was solicitous. He would murmur in my ear, "Does that hurt? Is that all right?" I would assure him that it wasn't painful, even if it was, because I loved him. I wanted him to have pleasure in his lifetime. After awhile I became quite accustomed to it and it was pleasure for me, also. When he reached the fullness of his pleasure, he used to buck and cry out like a horse being broken. I had a few concerns that others could hear him, but then realized that we were upstairs over the law firm and few residences were nearby.

I would use my mouth on him, also, and that was something in which he would take great pleasure as well. Sometimes he would turn me around on the bed and apply his mouth to me, but I think dutifully. It was not something he cared about, but he was a great democrat. Even if he founded the Republican party.

He was sexually adventurous. There was nothing of the prude about Abraham. He learned that if he put one finger inside me and then fondled me with his other hand, I found much pleasure in that. Particularly if he kissed me at the same time. After he had fulfilled himself upon my body he would then complete the exchange by handling me. I didn't suggest it. It was simply something we learned to do together.

Our relationship was very complete sexually and I think provided him with energy and sustenance through those difficult years of learning to be a lawyer and hoping for a future he had no way of knowing about. I always believed it was so unlikely my lover would become a president of this country that it had to be destined. God wished it to be. As God wished me to be a loving support in the early years. I never regretted that there was to be no more when he left Springfield. It was always evident to me that he was an unusual and supremely gifted person. I considered myself fortunate to have known the intimate side of this man at a time when he needed love.

He wrote to me rather frequently when we were separated and was as open in his letters as he was in person. I think he, too, felt I had been sent to him. He would say, "If human beings do it then it must be human." I'm sure he never suffered a moment of guilt or regret.

The last time I saw him, he was leaving Illinois for Washington to take his place at the head of the government. We had not been bed partners for some years then. I was married with my own business. I had children, as did he. I didn't particularly enjoy sleeping with my wife and I'm sure she didn't enjoy sleeping with me. But people do what they have to do. There was great regret in Abraham Lincoln's eyes. He had beautiful eyes, you know. A purply gray blue, with long eyelashes. Particularly on the lower edge. I always thought he was handsome. He shook my hand and embraced me. He said nothing. We were with other people and we never had talked about our affection for each other. I felt he knew he was not coming back. We didn't really imagine the horror of the Civil War coming, but there was a heavy feeling over the whole country. Something bad was coming; that was evident. And although becoming president of the United States was great prestige, great achievement, it was also like having been selected for ritual sacrifice on top of an Aztec pyramid. Your heart was to be cut out. Except very, very slowly day by day over a long period of time. Those who survive it without pain are those men who have no heart to cut out in the first place.

While Abraham Lincoln lay dying I read that the doctors, when they removed his clothes, marveled that he had the pale, strong body of a young man. His face became heavily lined through the years, but his body remained the same. I was comforted somehow.

Charles Herndon

The Trip to Bozeman

Dredging up the past isn't all fun, you know. The trip to Bozeman, Montana, could hardly come under the category of fun, although, as many people have said, "It seemed like a good idea at the time." Fred's brother Frank lived in Bozeman, where he worked. Doing what, I have no idea. Something to do with oil. Fred and Frank had agreed that Fred would buy Frank's car, and that Frank would come to San Francisco to fetch him in said car. A kind of grayish-blue Chevrolet, it turned out. And then we would return to Bozeman, where Frank would be dropped off and Fred would continue with the car to head east.

Fred and I bought that car together from Frank. I don't think Fred could have afforded it if we hadn't bought the car together. Could it have been as little as 600 dollars? I think it was. And we each put up 300 dollars.

The day came. Fred and I were now both out of the service. We hadn't fucked again since his crisis in my dreary rented apartment with the fold-down Murphy bed. But we had agreed to buy the car together and go to New York together, so what can I tell you?

Swarthy, Marlon Brando-ish Frank arrived from Bozeman with his girlfriend in tow. Red-haired Muriel. Muriel was no longer young, though I don't think Frank really registered that. Frank was tortured in some obscure way and had fled to Bozeman where the men outnumbered the women thirty-seven to one. Once I was told that, I quickly understood why Muriel was considered a hot ticket in Bozeman.

We ate with Frank and Muriel. We very likely showed them Fisherman's Wharf. Had a cocktail at the Top of the Mark, the bar on the highest floor of Mark Hopkins Hotel. Probably drove to Coit Tower to look out over the city. What is that strange quality in San Francisco that is so encapsulated in those little houses and streets on top of Telegraph Hill? There is never anyone walking in those treeless little streets that drop away between colorless, empty-windowed smallish buildings. Is there anyone within? Or are all that empty? With that same feeling your own apartment has when you drop in unexpectedly during the day when you should be at work. There is a grayness in the air, as though the apartment doesn't want you there. You are only supposed to be there in the evening and on weekends. Much of San Francisco has that feeling. As though the real residents are somewhere else and the whole city is waiting for their return.

It's a city something like one of those empty nests that a lazy bird has taken over. Or one of those seashells that are host to an itinerant slug once the original occupants have gone to their maker. Perhaps the big earthquake of 1906 did it. No one really believes the city is here to stay anymore.

We were not there to stay either, but left San Francisco early on a gray day. Were we carrying a lot of luggage? Is that why Muriel was alone in the backseat and I sat in front between Frank at the wheel and big, solid Fred? Now my memory fades, but certainly if there had been room I would have been in the backseat with Muriel. The ancient American tradition: the men together in front, the women in back.

I actually enjoyed that trip because I could rest my body against Fred's and no one was the wiser. It was sensual, whirling down the highway in that poky blue-gray car, Frank and Fred talking about their parents and family times back in Kansas. Muriel and I said little. I was half mesmerized with the road zooming under the front wheels of the car and the warmth of Fred beside me. He seemed to have no objection to my body resting against his.

We planned to drive through to Reno the first day, and it was already dark when we went over Donner Pass. It was spooky up there, the only car running through miles and miles of dank forest, fog drifting through the pines and across the road. When it came time to descend, it seemed that we went down and down for a very long time. Many, many miles. I thought of the Donner party stranded here in the deep snows, still so many miles from the valley on the other side of the mountains. What is so bad about eating other people, except for the fact that they're already dead? It's just meat. Eating a cow is really in no way different. The cow was once alive, too, and didn't want to die and certainly had no concept that it was there to provide food for human beings. What makes human beings so special that they should be entitled to eat other kinds of animals and not be eaten themselves? Tell that to a tiger. We're even picky about the kind of meat we're to eat. No horse, please. And we're not crazy about rabbits. Dogs and cats are a definite no-no. Except in a famine. It all seems terribly snobbish.

If we had gotten stranded, I would have preferred to eat Frank. He seemed like he would make a more solid, steaklike kind of meal. I wouldn't have liked Muriel. Flabby. And I would never have taken a bite of my darling Fred. I don't think. Although I would have been glad to have provided some solid meals for my starving honey, if it had come to that.

Those were my thoughts as we coasted down the mountainside for what seemed to be halfway across the state of California. Soon we were at the state line of Nevada. And there in a small building precisely on the line was an array of one-armed bandits. Drivers were leaping from their cars to run in and start on their addiction. We remained in our car, but Muriel and Frank rushed to lose money as soon as we were in Reno. We found a motel, left our luggage, and although it was already midnight, went downtown. In the first casino, Muriel marched up to the front row of machines and started hurling her quarters in. I think this was perhaps her whole reason for coming on the trip. These stolen moments in Reno.

Fred and I left Frank attached to a blackjack table and walked about. Patti Page was appearing in the main room of the club—could it have been Harrah's? Patti singing "How Much Is That Doggy in the Window?" was an event I was more than happy to miss. I was not without sophistication even then. Fortunately we had just missed the last show.

Reno was a strange town in those days. Perhaps still is. The large neon signs lit up the casinos as though something were actually going on. But one block away behind the lights there was nothing but one-story buildings on treeless streets and the desert calling just one block farther out. A very emotional city. There was really nothing there except neon and greed.

Fred was reluctant to leave Frank and Muriel, so I left him in the casino and took a cab back to our motel. I tried to sleep but didn't manage very much until they crawled in a few hours later and Fred had come to share the double bed I was in.

In those years not so long ago, if two couples rented a motel suite with two double beds, they used them as such. And if one of the couples were both men, no one thought anything of their sharing a bed. It was probably a decade later, in the decadent 1960s, that the public woke up to the fact that if two men were in bed together there might be hanky-panky. We have Mick Jagger to thank for that.

Fred threw himself under the thin covers and backed up against my body, turned away from him. He threw an arm backward over me to pull me tightly against him and back to back we were soon asleep.

The next day, Fred and I left Muriel and Frank entombed in the casinos and went to Silver City to see where the beautifully dressed Lucius Beebe had disported himself for many years in the 1930s and 1940s. I had often read of Lucius in magazines when I was a child and knew that he was an elegant man-about-town who escorted debutantes to first-night openings in New York and hung around at the Stork Club and El Morocco. And that he had taken a private railway car and a friend and gone to live in Silver City.

There wasn't much to Silver City except a main street with a couple of ramshackle saloons and a large wooden opera house. I suppose stars of the mining period like Lotta Crabtree performed there. It must have been relatively easy to be a star in those days. Just physically getting yourself somewhere like Silver City in a stagecoach must have guaranteed an enthusiastic reception.

I tried to imagine the street full of jostling miners and now-disappeared wooden houses covering the barren landscape around Silver City, but it didn't happen.

Luscious Lucius had left no glamorous imprint on Silver City, and I could see no sign where his private railroad car might have been. Did he go there to get away from it all with his "friend," of whom very little was said?

It was a high-skyed, gray day when we visited Silver City and another wide-open and empty day followed as we departed for Bozeman. Did we make that drive all in one day? I don't remember stopping another night, so it's very likely we again drove straight through, arriving late.

As we approached Bozeman in the night, it seemed to be a vast city with lights spreading across the land for miles in every direction. But Frank explained that these were only oil rigs.

There was a five-story hotel in Bozeman and we had lunch at its rooftop restaurant the next day. This was where the movers and shakers of Bozeman met for what would later be called power lunches. I think I had a bacon, lettuce, and tomato sandwich, which was much like the same sandwich all over the country. Which was what I liked about it.

Again, there were few trees in Bozeman, but the buildings were of brick here and there and it had a certain solidity. On the street I saw a girl I had known vaguely in college. A large dark-haired solidly built girl with dark rings around her eyes. She had some kind of reputation as an intellectual at the university, I think. She must have been lured to Bozeman by its reputation of thirty-seven men to each woman. But it appeared not even that had worked for her. She looked alone and lonely and very out of place in her plaid skirt and dark sweater here among the cowpokes and the tumble weed. I felt a pang for her. Perhaps she's still there, now married and the mother of many. Grandmother of many, perhaps. I hope so.

We stayed in Bozeman several days, Fred and I sleeping on a foldout couch in Frank's living room. The night before we left, Frank gave a cocktail party. A real cocktail party and quite a few folks turned out.

Fred and I had gone to church the day before. It was my wont to attend church weekly as I had been brought up to do. At the service in the small church in Bozeman, which was surely one of several, I noticed that every woman there wore a dark mink coat. There was money for mink in Bozeman and church was probably one of the few places to flaunt it.

A lot of monied folk turned out for Frank's party. He seemed to be a lot better connected socially than one might have expected from his surly manner and flannel shirts. Muriel emerged for the party. She had been very absent since our arrival in town. She even looked somewhat chic in black velvet and confided in me, "You were so funny during the trip from San Francisco I could hardly keep from laughing." I was reassured that my attempts at being amusing during that endless trip across the plains had not been entirely wasted.

In the morning as we were waking up, Fred fucked me and then was angry about it. Was I going to say no just because we were in a fold-out bed in his brother's living room? I would have had sex with him standing up in a glass phone booth.

When we pushed the curtains open we discovered that it had snowed all night, even though it was nearly April. Bozeman was snowbound. We walked down to a coffee shop where Fred glowered at his cup and the tabletop and was very sulky. But the sun came out and we decided to venture forth toward Ogallala, Nebraska. The snow was light on the roads, even though no snowplows were in evidence. By noon Fred had gotten over his chagrin at having fucked in his brother's living room and had regained his good spirits.

Did we stay overnight in Ogallala? I think not, as I remember sailing through a ghostly small town lit by occasional streetlights under tall cottonwood trees, almost a mirage in the endless plains that slid slightly downhill all the way to the Mississippi. We may very well have just driven through the night until we reached the small town in Kansas where Fred had been brought up. His father was genial. His brother (this brother was named Phil) seemed suspicious. And his mother was ghostly. There was something very Southern about both the little town and his mother, who seemed to be always upstairs resting. She was almost like ectoplasm, appearing at the foot of the stairs smiling wearily and then disappearing upward. Tennessee Williams was from St. Louis, so all that weird stuff may come from farther afield than Mississippi and New Orleans.

You wonder, don't you, if all these lovely women found the act of sexual intercourse so different from romance that they just had to go find some other world to inhabit? I certainly have, but I've gotten used to it.

We drove about and visited Fred's high school friends and I could see him as the big, friendly football player they all knew. If I had been a girl we probably would have been announcing our engagement. I don't remember ever wishing that were the case. I was perfectly happy, even thrilled, that my big handsome Fred was coming with me to New York where we were going to fuck our brains out. Which, despite his protestations, is what Fred had in mind, too, I believe.

Fred stayed behind and I flew back to Illinois to spend a week with my family before we went on to New York. Fred was going to drive up with our jointly owned car and fetch me.

Uncle Guy and Aunt May visited while I was at home. From Bloomington, Indiana, I returned to Springfield with them to rendezvous with Fred, to shorten the drive a little for him. He arrived at Guy and May's house in early evening and I fixed him something to eat in their kitchen. They seemed wary of Fred and didn't seem to want to make his acquaintance. They stayed out of the kitchen and were formal when we left for my home in Illinois. Like Fred's brother Phil, they seemed to sense that there was more to this relationship than met the eye. They were actually seasoned travelers and Uncle Guy had worked in the foreign service. Perhaps the very fact that I had come down to meet Fred aroused their suspicions. I had been brought up to think that anything my family did was all right, so even though I sensed their coolness I dismissed it as being unworthy of notice. Which is exactly what anyone else in my family would have done. Uncle Guy was my mother's uncle, in fact, and although she loved him I think she cared nothing for his opinion and thought he had lost status in marrying Aunt May, who was not beautiful and still had a countrified accent.

We arrived very late at my home. I took the wheel to roll through the night, one country town after another. No people on the streets. Few cars. Only a kind of darkness that seemed clearer and shinier than the darkness of the plains that we had crossed. I always felt better when I was with Fred, so I felt now our true voyage together was starting, even though my mother had made it clear that Fred was to occupy his own bedroom. She had once said to me when I was a teenager, "You are so friendly and cooperative it's a good thing you're not a girl or you'd be pregnant all the time." Perhaps she understood more than we ever discussed, or it was her subconscious speaking.

I showed Fred to his room in the silent house where everyone normally retired to their rooms at ten o'clock to read and then dream. The next morning we departed for New York. I had no desire to show Fred around my hometown and introduce him to my friends and family. They didn't interest me and I was sure they wouldn't interest him. Also, to be honest, I was well aware that I had been an officer in the navy and Fred had been an enlisted man. If that had come up in conversation, it would have been something they would never have understood. It has become increasingly clear to me as time passes that sexual relationships are never as important to other people as social relationships.

What Is It About the Nature of Love?

What is it about the nature of love? There's always something sordid about it. Some dark little secret; being in love with someone you shouldn't be.

Hankering after your father or a hired man.

Longing to be held against some baroque chest by huge arms because no one cuddled you enough. And now you can never get enough cuddling and coddling to the end of your days.

And what about those oak-barrel-built guys? Why are they so romantic? With no equipment to be romantic with; nothing they've read; nothing they've heard sung, nothing. But still they long for you. Like some big, brown-eyed bullock with dull, little gray wives by their sides, they stand stolidly and long to have you grab them and make their lives into some kind of magic they can't even imagine. Complaining every foot of the way.

And your job is to never let them push you into being the gray little wife. The one the neighbors can never complain about. Your job is to lure them down that path to the dark, little secret so they can groan aloud in the night and get it out of their system, that thing they don't even know enough about to be able to discuss.

So what if you laugh too much? And cry too easily? I think they fall in love with you because you're not afraid of falling in love and they are.

NEW YORK

The Trip to Putnam Hill

From Illinois Fred and I decided to go to New York through Canada to add another country to our travels. From there Fred and I were planning to make a stop at an uncle and aunt's country house in Putnam Hill, about two hours north of New York City. And then we would go on to the city with them.

Perhaps one reason we left my hometown with no delay was to arrive at Putnam Hill during a weekend when Uncle Anchor and Aunt Alice would be there. Uncle Anchor was my mother's brother. Anchor had been my mother's maiden name. It was not to suggest that he was to be the mainstay of the family, although that was very much the case.

Fred and I nipped across Canada, so flat, so bleak. There must be something about that terrain that produces flat, bleak people.

Once we found our way through the inexplicable highways around Buffalo, we were in the hills and dales of the Finger Lakes region of upper New York State. For those who never crossed the country before superhighways were in place, much has been missed. There was no boredom on the highways when they were only two lanes wide and loaded with cars and trucks. Through the Finger Lakes we repeatedly passed all the trucks going uphill and the trucks repeatedly passed us going downhill. Since there was little else but one hilltop after another, every driver got to see a lot of the other cars and trucks on the highway.

It was thrilling, it was tiring, and Fred and I were glad to lay our heads down in an auto court near Canandaigua. My ancestors had come to Illinois from this countryside, but I cared nothing for that. We were on our way to New York City and an exciting life lay in wait. I didn't allow myself to feel any qualms or misgivings. I was older than Fred by two years and it was up to me to forge ahead. Also, Fred already had a job in a stock brokerage firm arranged by his father, who had old friends in New York. I had Aunt Alice and Uncle Anchor and, although I had no plans to work for them nor wished to, I knew they would be of help in finding a job. I had very little idea as to what I wanted to do. I really didn't care. I just wanted to earn a living and be with Fred. Isn't it strange how things work out?

I think Fred liked me. I think he loved me early on but quickly saw that screwing me wasn't going to fit in with the lifestyle that was destined to unfold before him. Yet he had a strong sense of responsibility. He wasn't about to dump me, particularly when I clung to him in the night crying and saying, "Please don't leave me, not yet. Not quite yet." I really needed Fred; there were no two ways about it.

But there was no touching or fondling. Fred was again turning over a new leaf that night on the road. And I guess I had some pride. Scorn was more like it. I wasn't going to grovel to have the sex that he enjoyed as much as I did.

When we arrived at Putnam Hill after lunchtime on the second day of our trip, Fred was impressed. I don't think anything about me impressed him as much as the home of my aunt and uncle did.

It was a beautiful house that had been built on a hillside overlooking the Berkshire Mountains and the valley below. A rather original house for people of their conservative and arriviste tastes. They had both come from solid but unassuming backgrounds. Now they lived among state governors, internationally famous newscasters (two of them!), a Kennedy sister and her cute husband, and titles and movie stars drifted in and out with regularity. They had become as elegant as the people they knew and were extremely popular for their high spirits and hospitality.

Their home had a very traditional New England facade of white frame with green shutters. But when we stepped through the door we entered a wide foyer of pale wood with broad steps leading down to a living room that was the entire first floor, with what was certainly the first picture window in that part of the woods. We felt that we were stepping outside again, the gigantic window framing the green lawns that swept down to the hay meadows below and then across treetops to the distant mountains, always a little smoky in the haze that hung in the air over the valley. Pawling was down there, a curious little place in which the train tracks ran through the center of town. One of my aunt's neighbors tried to cross the street by passing through the train while it was standing in the station and was swept off to nearby Patterson, where she had to take a taxi back to Pawling.

Entering this room with its overwhelming view, Fred knew he was somewhere different. My Aunt Alice was from a farm in western Kansas in her very distant past, so she immediately favored Fred. My Uncle Anchor wasn't any more aloof with him than he was with me, which was pretty aloof. I couldn't do anything for Uncle Anchor, so I wasn't of great interest.

Fred and I were put in the maid's quarters, which was fine with me. Aunt Alice always traveled with a maid, who also cooked a bit, but didn't like being in the separated back wing alone, I guess. So Margaret the maid had the green bedroom upstairs, down the hall from Aunt Alice and Uncle Anchor. The smallest of the guest rooms. Minor guests were then put in her ground floor room beyond the kitchen.

Aunt Alice had a blue bedroom, a yellow bedroom, and a green bedroom on the upper floor. Her own suite was pink. Pink, pink, pink. I don't think she wanted to look in a mirror in her own bedroom unless she was surrounded with pink to make her look as fresh as possible.

There were twin beds in the maid's room in the back wing, which suited Fred just fine. After we unpacked I took him for a drive. I had lived there one summer with Aunt Alice and Uncle Anchor, so I knew my way around Putnam Hill. We drove down by the lake where I had gone every day to sun and swim in the summer. Then to the crest of the hill where fine mansions lined themselves up in white Victorian correctness with a quarter mile of lawn between each one. From there past the country club and the golf course that crested one of the outlying shoulders of the hill.

We went over to the very New Englandy church where everyone assembled on Sunday morning, no matter the state of their soul or what religion they may have originally embraced. And we came back on the old Post Road. At one time a stagecoach wandered along just below the crest of Putnam Hill, connecting distant communities. Why it didn't thread through the valley I don't know. There had been a huge frame resort hotel where the church now stood. Perhaps the Post Road led there. Now the road was long deserted and wound through deep forest in two rutted tracks. If another car was coming from the other direction you had trouble avoiding each other. Someone had to pull over into the underbrush.

The Post Road was a shortcut back to my aunt and uncle's house and we generally used it on Sunday mornings only, but I drove Fred through it to give him the complete tour.

Putnam Hill was beautiful in the May weather, like an Emily Dickinson poem, all wildflowers and blowing grass, very green trees with black trunks, and always damp. Rot was only a moment away on Putnam Hill. Fred loved it. Kansas was nothing like the hill, and covered as it was with glamorous people, I think he began to have some real enthusiasm for our adventure to New York.

In the morning as I was getting ready to take a bath, I saw him lying in his bed eyeing me ruminatively. I turned on the bathtub, took off my pajamas, and, leaning over the tub with my hand on the tap, looked back out the door to his bed. "Come in here," I said. I was thinking that if my aunt or the maid suddenly entered our room, which wasn't out of the question, we could both be in the bathroom with the tub running. Locking the bedroom door would immediately cause suspicion. I wasn't about to do that.

Fred got out of bed. We both wore pajamas that I had bought at Brooks Brothers. He had started wearing his now that he was no longer in the navy. He had an erection.

He dropped his pajamas as he crossed the room, and by the time he came into the bathroom he was naked. His body of a river god always excited me. White and fleshy and full. The large thighs, large pectoral muscles, large biceps, rounded and smooth and hairless. He had short blond curls all over his head and around his penis. He was my god and looked it.

Fred pushed the door shut. He understood the drill. And leaned over my back. The running water covered any noise as he entered and with his upper body clinging to me moved his hips vigorously in and out. Actually Fred enjoyed fucking very much and he wasn't eager to get it over with. We hadn't had intercourse since his brother's couch in far-away Bozeman, so there was reason for him to be in the mood. It wasn't all that much fun for me, bracing myself against the slippery tub and keeping an eye on the spigot, but as always with Fred, his pleasure was my pleasure. And it was pleasing. He came, letting his arms drop and resting against my back. Then pulled out and left the bathroom.

I took a bath in the water that now filled the tub. I didn't hurry. When I came out he was back in his bed with the covers half over him. He looked at me balefully. The sorceress had lured him into having sex again. He was pissed off. I ignored him. I certainly wasn't going to stop having sex with him. There were limits to what I was willing to do to make him feel good.

Fred took a bath. We joined my uncle and aunt at the octagonal table for brunch at one end of the living room. Margaret the maid joined us as there were no other guests. Aunt Alice was very democratic. Margaret always joined us at the table unless there were guests to be served.

In the evening we all went into New York together, Fred and I in the backseat of Uncle Anchor's car. We left our little gray-blue car in the parking space in front of the country house. We were going to stay at their apartment until we found one of our own. Margaret we dropped off at the Pawling train station to return separately so we wouldn't be too crowded in the car. She probably hated us.

Aunt Alice and Uncle Anchor lived in a vast apartment just off Fifth Avenue in the Seventies. The building had been built for a nineteenth-century publishing tycoon and looked like a Venetian palace. Huge stone pillars across the second floor gave it the appearance of a bank. The apartment was on the second floor with a balcony behind the pillars. The living room was two stories high and of gigantic proportions. And deathly still. It was all in sapphire blue, with white satin couches facing each other in front of the fireplace. A large painting of Aunt Alice in white satin hung over it. She had been very beautiful. It was not hard to understand why Uncle Anchor had left his first wife for her. Although such things were never done in our family. Or hers. Now they seemed very removed from such shenanigans, and Aunt Alice's relationship with my cousins would never have suggested that she was not their own mother. They loved her as everyone did. Their own mother, Aunt Lucille, was harder to love.

Between the enormous living room and the enormous bedroom to the rear of the apartment was a smaller two-story section. The kitchen was below the heavy wood staircase that rose up there, and two smallish bedrooms were above for guests, with an adjoining bathroom. Through the windows of those rooms came the very distinctive smell of New York. The smell of car exhaust and tired trees and millions of people. Fred moved far from me in the double bed. I didn't care. We were in New York. I was in New York. With a man I loved and high adventure lay ahead. I was thrilled to lie there and hear the traffic roaring on Fifth Avenue in the night, the streetlight fading its way through the musty draperies and across the bed. I wasn't sure that I even wanted Fred's arms around me. That would probably happen in the night.

Some Men Who Slept with Other Men, No. 3*

I SLEPT WITH DWIGHT EISENHOWER

The first thing you should know is that he had a beautiful body. Of all the Eisenhower boys, he was by far the best-looking. Milton wasn't bad-looking but he was never sexy.

Dwight was a football star. And he had worked hard all his life as a kid, so he was strong. With broad shoulders and a narrow waist. I think later people got all caught up with that bald head and the big grin. He wasn't like that at all when I knew him in high school. He was good-tempered but he wasn't all charm and smiles. He was even kind of sulky.

He was always good at sports and quite an outdoorsman. Lots of hunting, shooting, camping. That sort of thing. Not that Abilene, Kansas, was much on wildlife and the great outdoors. God, it was dry most of the time. But we did have the Smoky Hill River where we could shoot ducks and catch fish.

Ike was from the south side of Abilene and I was from the north side. We got to know each other when they built the new high school in 1904. We never really thought much about being rich or poor. But the north side was where the bankers and lawyers lived. My father was a doctor. He had built one of those big wooden Victorian monstrosities when I was little and we lived there with a boy to take care of the yard and a hired girl. We had some means. But Dwight's family on the south side was crowded into a much smaller house. There were very few trees and lawns over there.

We were both on the football team and in those group showers you got a chance to size the other guys up as far as their bodies and their

---

*One last story written for hesitant Fred.

equipment go. I don't know what it is with homosexual men like myself, but we seem to have a weakness for men who look like Greek gods. And he did. He had broad shoulders and strong legs and lots of muscles. Not so very tall but very well proportioned. And blond. He was quite something. And quite a sizable thing down there dangling between his legs also. What is it about blond pubic hair? He was a little godlet.

We went camping with our pals and you know how boys are. There's always a lot of horsing around and comparing penis sizes and the occasional circle jerk. But Ike and I had something. We particularly liked being together. He never really had a girlfriend in high school. He liked Ruby Norman but I think more as a pal. High school isn't really where your sex drive comes raging out. It's more about being popular and looking good in the eyes of the other boys. Ruby was red-headed and fun and I think Ike liked her for that. And in those days there was very little hands-on entertainment. We didn't have cars then and there was just so much that could go on sitting in the front-porch swing with parents peering through the front window at regular intervals.

But when we were out camping alone along the river, we could get all our clothes off and fool around. I don't know. I suppose when you're fourteen, fifteen, and sixteen you sort of want to do things that feel good and are exciting. It doesn't occur to you that maybe this is the way things will be for the rest of your life. Which is how it turned out for me.

It was very different for Ike. He was at heart a very romantic and loving kind of person. And in that mob of kids his mother had I don't think he ever got enough affection. I realized that it wasn't just kids fooling around when I started wanting him to kiss me on those overnight camping trips. And I got him to enter me. Me lying face down on an old Indian blanket. Him on top of me. When he was about to come, he would pull my head around and kiss me at the same time. We actually did a lot of stuff. I sat on him. And we did some sixty-nining. I don't think he was ever into that very much, but he was adventurous and willing to try things.

There was a kind of girlie side to Dwight, too, that I don't think anyone else ever saw. When we sat around the campfire, even with a bunch of other boys, he liked to lean back against me and have me put my arms around him. We had never heard the word "queer" in those days, so boys putting their arms around each other meant nothing.

We slept together from time to time right up until he left for West Point. He had a friend, Swede Hazlett, who was planning to go to Annapolis and got Ike all fired up about trying to go. Ike was out of high school and working nights at the creamery to earn money to send his brother Edgar to the University of Michigan. They had made a deal that each would work a year while the other went to college until they both had graduated. It was going to take them eight years, but that was the plan. Then Swede Hazlett came into the picture and Ike decided to try to get a free education at the military's cost. Lo and behold, he did it.

I like to think that maybe Ike's sex life with me was the best, or at least the most exploratory, of his life. He married Mamie and after their first child died I think their physical relationship became very routine. I read in his biography that he only tried to have sex once with his female driver during the war. And couldn't get it up. Some guys are so nice they can't even get a hard-on.

So there you have my sex life with Dwight Eisenhower, famous general and president. I never saw him again after he left Abilene. I left, too, and spent the rest of my life in Chicago. But I read about him and saw his picture in the papers constantly. Many are the times I remember that muscular warm body of his pressed against mine while the campfire was flickering out. It's one of the most beautiful memories I have. I hope that it meant a little something to him and that from time to time he remembered.

Orin Anderson

Patchin Place

We found an apartment in Greenwich Village, but it wasn't easy. Before leaving San Francisco, a girl I knew who took wedding photos and was on her way to being a lesbian gave me the name of a friend in New York. The friend worked in a Greenwich Village real estate company. And she found us the little apartment in Patchin Place.

Do you know Patchin Place? A little row of brick houses painted gray, standing along a narrow passage full of ailanthus trees. A gate stands at the entrance to this tiny street, which is surrounded by the backs of houses facing on Greenwich and Sixth Avenue.

What could these houses have been, three little stories and two little rooms on each floor? Perhaps they were servants' quarters originally. Or a pre-Revolution real estate development on a modest scale. Very modest.

We had the second floor at Number One. There was no double bed, which neither of us complained about. Now that we were in New York, two men sleeping in a double clearly would have been suspect. We took turns sleeping in the little bedroom on the single bed, the other using the daybed in the living room under the windows. The living room also included a fireplace on one wall and a small upright piano on the other. When we had friends to dinner we opened a card table between the piano and the fireplace. Whoever was to eat sitting on the daybed had to go there before the table was opened, as there was no room to pass through afterward.

There was also a large butterfly chair, one of those iron-framed contraptions with a black canvas seat. The canvas had pockets that hooked over the four curved projections of the frame, making a low-slung kind of sitting-up hammock. I wonder if these chairs exist anymore. They were the forerunners of the beanbag chair and every bit as uncomfortable.

What else? A tiny kitchen so dirty I painted it white and then hand-painted little blue flowers all over the walls and ceiling. I wonder if those hand-painted little flowers are still there. Not impossible in Greenwich Village, where redecoration is not a high priority.

Behind the kitchen was an equally small bathroom. The bathroom tub slanted downhill toward the corner where the floor sank. After bathing we had to scoop the water uphill toward the drain with our hands to empty the tub.

The windows on the front looked into the low-hanging trees drooping over the courtyard. Little sun filtered into Patchin Place, but at night the light from Tenth Street reached our windows, and when we made love on the daybed I could see Fred's pale, strongly rounded body in the dim light.

Shortly after we moved in, a navy friend was in town and I invited him to stay with us. To sleep where? Perhaps we had a folding cot. He had brought a girl to have dinner with us and, while he was walking her to the nearby subway station, Fred wanted sex. I was already lying on the daybed when he came out of the bathroom naked. For the first time he climbed on top of me and settled his buttocks down on my erect penis. He had never done that before, though I had ridden him to orgasm a number of times. While he was seated on me he masturbated.

The navy friend had already been gone about twenty minutes and the subway station was only about a five-minute walk away. Fred still hadn't reached orgasm, although he was bucking and pulling frantically, his head thrown back, when I heard the gate clang shut at the courtyard entrance. Then the friend's footsteps as he approached the front door. He had a key.

As his steps started up the stairs, Fred came profusely over my chest and stomach. As the key turned in the lock he pulled off me and I pulled the covers up as he disappeared into the bathroom. Just then John David entered the darkness of the room. I said calmly, "I just got into bed. Fred's in the bathroom. I put a towel in the bathroom for you." Fred emerged from the bathroom his big, jovial self and said good night. Who would imagine that moments before he had been sweating and groaning over my body? In many ways Fred was a much

better dissembler than I was. His football player demeanor put the lie
to any errant thoughts that he and I might be lovers.

I cooked in that little apartment. A range of dishes my mother had
taught me. Little meals for bachelors. Chile con carne made from Campbell's tomato soup and canned beans with real hamburger and poured
over noodles. Also a kind of tuna dish that involved mixing canned
tuna and Campbell's mushroom soup and pouring that over noodles.
I served noodles so often that guests referred to the wicker clothes
hamper in the bathroom as the "noodle locker," assuming that somewhere in the apartment there was a large storage place for the noodles.

I don't remember Fred in the little kitchen. I did bacon and eggs
very well. And the butcher in San Diego who had taught me to cook
liver and bacon in a way that avoided that uriney taste had done a
good job. We often had liver. I had quite a repertoire. None of which I
have cooked in years.

I never had dreams of domesticity there in the tiny apartment with
Fred. I was going uptown to my advertising job that Aunt Alice had
helped me find.

There I wore a smart new wardrobe from Brooks Brothers, made
friends, and went out to nightclubs a lot in the evening. You could go
out to clubs like the Purple Onion, the Page Three, the Blue Note
where George Shearing played. Even on our minuscule salaries we
managed to be out and about New York a great deal.

Some of my friends from the navy were in New York. Herb and
Doug and Mitch. There were new wives and spooky apartments like
ours, and it was fun. We smoked, we drank, we were witty. In the
nightclubs we talked a lot and weren't very polite to the entertainment. But then no one was. That was what nightclubbing was all
about. Smoky rooms and clinking drinks and the buzz of talk and
laughter over the music. Coming out into the warm night and laughing good-bye and singing or throwing up in a taxi on the way downtown.

And then into our dark apartment where we could throw our
clothes off and fall into each other's arms and feel each other's warm
bodies and damp kisses and explore each other's intimate crevices.

We were young. We hadn't done everything by then. We didn't know yet what we would like and what we wouldn't like. I wanted to find out and I had big, handsome Fred to help me. The handsomest man in the world, big and strong and blond, climbing on my body, placing me on top of his body. Far from his family, Fred explored right along with me and even led me into areas I wouldn't have thought of myself in the dark of Patchin Place. But in the daylight he felt fear as he orbited away from the world he knew.

What I remember most of all of that summer Fred and I had in New York is the early evenings. A smell in the air that is only New York which you get used to and don't notice unless you've been gone a very long time.

What's it like? Automobile exhaust, of course. Mixed with the smell of foliage and trees that have been gasping for air for years. And perhaps the fragrance of all the bodies moving through the thick, hot air of New York in the summer. And the fragrances those bodies wore: Ma Griffe, Jungle Gardenia, Bellodgia, Femme, Jolie Madame, Diorissimo, and the men's Canoe and Old Spice, of course. Russian Leather, too.

Walking down Christopher Street at the end of the day, having come out of the hot and crowded subway at Sheridan Square, the air under the high trees was gray already with the fading of the day. The Hudson River was near—perhaps there is the smell of the sea and salt in the odor that is so particularly New York. And the sky to the west was lighter with the reflection of the broad river and the sun that was still over New Jersey.

All the house fronts were worn and shabby. Lights were already on behind the windows, but there was energy. Lives were being lived to their owners' satisfaction.

Almost everywhere in the United States, dusk is sad. It certainly was in Illinois. At home I used to sit in the middle of the couch and cry for no reason. Other than that there was no life there. I wonder if it was as sad for the Indians as they cruised over the prairies or sat on the shores. There *is* something eternally sad, as though something is missing, about the great American landscapes at the end of the day. But not in New York. There the end of the day was romantic and full of promise.

Through the shadows under the trees, through the warm, stinky fragrance of the night, I was walking to a little brick row house where Fred would be waiting. His thick thighs would be spread as he lounged in the black butterfly chair reading the paper. Waiting for me to prepare some kind of noodle something and then we could wander off into the night, perhaps around the corner to Chumley's, the former speakeasy. Or down the street to Marie's Crisis, or the peppy Arthur's Tavern, or plunge down the stairs into the rowdy Five Oaks. And then home for a really good fuck on the narrow bed in the tiny bedroom. I was living my fantasies. What a lucky fellow I was.

A Little Trip to Washington

One of my friends in New York was Marion Padwee. We had gone to university together in Illinois. Marion was a tall girl with gracious manners and an edge of nervousness. Men who dated her at school had called her Panic-Button Padwee. In what way she was panicky I don't know, except perhaps she wasn't eager to have her underwear explored in the backseat of a car. I, of course, would have been delighted to have my underwear torn off and thrown out the window by some college athlete, so there was little for Marion and I to share there.

Perhaps I overstate. At eighteen or nineteen I might have been a little gun-shy of being pawed over, even if cooperative.

At twenty-six, when Marion and I met once again, I was more seasoned. And Marion seemed to be, too. She now worked at a women's magazine and wore tight sleeveless black linen sheath dresses (I suppose she really only had one but that seemed to be how she was always dressed). Her hair was pulled back tautly into a short ponytail. The inevitable correct look of the postdeb in New York, imitated perfectly by all the girls who were never considered "cute" in the Midwest and came to New York to discover they could be chic.

Fred and I liked to hang around with Marion because she did not seem to be obviously looking for a man. At least she wasn't interested in Fred, and I was old stuff. What dear innocent years those were, in the 1950s. The fact that Fred and I lived together and were always together wherever we went and never dated women piqued no one's interest or curiosity. There must have been tons of guys like us around New York in those days. Some gay and getting it on. Some just old school or military pals who liked living together. Hardly anyone seemed to live alone. So Fred and I were rather lost in the shuffle.

Fred enjoyed socializing with women, and Marion and he had a kind of joshing and kidding around manner with each other that suited both of them. So when I thought it would be fun to take a drive down to Washington for a weekend, it seemed entirely suitable to invite Marion along. Maybe we needed a third person to be more amusing for one another.

Why do I remember this trip? Did I think of these projects to keep Fred amused? More likely I just liked rambling about, he had never been to the capital, and so we departed. There was a certain excollegiate style to our lives. Just dashing here and there, drinking a little too much, looking smart. That's what young people did then. The 1960s hadn't happened yet. We weren't trying to find ourselves. We didn't feel at all lost. Of course Jack Kerouac and Allen Ginsberg and that crowd were around somewhere but we knew nothing of them. Young working professionals in New York would never have crossed paths with them. And we wouldn't have liked them much if we had. We would have thought that they took themselves much too seriously.

How long could the drive to Washington have taken? Fred and I had found a garage for the car at the end of a subway line in the Bronx. Our weekend routine was to take the subway out there, pick up the car, and head off in one direction or another. Many other people must have done much the same thing, as the streets around the subway station were lined with rows of wooden garages. We probably took Marion with us to the Bronx and then crossed the Hudson and headed south. The New Jersey Turnpike existed then, so we would have made good time to Philadelphia, and then headed on down past Baltimore to Washington.

We stayed in a guest house once we arrived in Washington. It was evening when we arrived and how we knew where to look I have no idea. But many faded and well-bred ladies used their homes as guest houses in those days. You rang the bell and the owner, nicely dressed and hair in place despite the hour, answered the door and you were shown bedrooms. I don't remember that we shopped around much or looked at the rooms first. We wouldn't have. We were all too well bred, also. And the rooms were always the same. Just like my grandmother's guest room. The large double bed with a dark wooden headboard and knobs on the footboard. The dark bureau with a rectangular mirror on the back. A little armchair upholstered in cretonne. They called that a "slipper chair." To sit on while you donned your slippers? A faded oriental carpet, perhaps real, perhaps not. And always yellowish walls. Probably cream originally. The windows had flimsy curtains pulled back on either side with a pull-down window shade in the same aged cream as the walls. And the same musty smell. In a guest house these rooms must have been occupied very regularly, but they always smelled as though they hadn't been opened for years.

We were tired, Fred and I. I think he may well have driven all the way. I hated to drive. So there was no hanky-panky. And in the morning we were up and out of there after sharing the bathroom in the hall. It was fun and easy, because of the innocence. The landlady took it as a matter of course that Fred and I would share a double bed. It had been that way since deep in the nineteenth century. Herman Melville's Ishmael shared a bed with Queequeg. Nathaniel Hawthorne slept with his Uncle Robert until he was fifteen. Lucky uncle. Nathaniel was a cutie. Did you know that?

So Fred and I bundled into our double bed and out again in the morning. Leaving it for the maid to make. We would be back to stay another night after checking out the monuments.

Something has been spoiled about summer by air-conditioning. Washington wasn't air-conditioned in the 1950s. Neither was New York. Where I worked on Park Avenue, the windows of the offices opened to let the warm air pour in. In my little interior office with no windows there was a fan fastened high on the wall. When the temperature got to ninety-six degrees everyone was sent home.

My dentist still has his offices in one of those buildings. Every time I use his bathroom I open the window and look out over Madison Avenue from the twentieth floor. It takes me back to the days before air-conditioning. Of course those windows were an invitation to suicide, but I never heard of anyone flinging himself out.

Air-conditioning seems to shut us away not only from the heat but also from our emotions. Like television, everything is always on the other side of the glass.

But on that hot Washington day we drove about with all the car windows down. Fred and I wore short-sleeved white shirts, I'm sure.

Or perhaps mine was a plaid shirt, in that Indian cloth, what was it called? Madras. It was new that year from Brooks Brothers. They did shorts and long pants in the same fabric, always in plaid. It was considered daring, a little fruity, but cutting edge for men's fashion. We wore dark gray flat front pants or suntans (now they call them khakis) with them. And Bermuda shorts weren't out of the question. Some daring men wore them on the streets of Manhattan with dark knee socks and jacket and tie. I never went that far.

Marion would have had one of those standard tight, sleeveless dresses. Her bare elbow would rest on a window opening. The wind would blow in the sleeves of our shirts when Fred and I would do the same. Billowing out our shirts and cooling us off. The T-shirt was still considered underwear pretty much, unless you were washing the car and paired it with old navy dungarees.

We cruised around Washington, two short-haired young men and a young woman with a side part and hair just above her shoulders.

Marion would complain a little that the wind was blowing her hair out of its pageboy. She said, "My hair is fine. So fine." Fred said, "Your hair is perfectly fine." And we all laughed. Fred wasn't often witty and he was as surprised as Marion and I were that he had been funny. We said, "Your hair is perfectly fine" the rest of the summer and laughed a lot when no one else saw anything funny. Being witty was important then, and we liked referring to wittiness of the past that was part of our own personal history and made no sense to others.

The Lincoln Memorial stands out most in my mind. The brooding quality of that figure back in the shadows of the temple. It made me feel that something bad had happened that was not easily forgiven. There is an upside to memories of Washington, the father of our country, and the big stone penis straining toward the sky is probably apt as an expression of the time when we said "fuck you" to England. But there is no upside to the Civil War and Lincoln's assassination. That is just one long sadness. I felt that standing on the marble steps looking up into the darkness at that mourning face.

We didn't visit the White House. It seemed small there, standing behind its iron fence across the lawns. I had seen pictures. I didn't particularly care about seeing those stupid rooms done up in colors no one would ever have in their home. Brilliant blue. Bright green. Shiny red. Whose fault was that? Dolly Madison? And the furniture is really ugly. Blocky and heavy and covered in gold-leafed eagles. Where did ideas like that about interior decoration come from?

The entire day felt as though we were somehow underwater. That damp, warm air and the heavy smell of the foliage and trees everywhere, making the air pale green.

By the latter part of the afternoon Fred said he was going to have a drink and, since there were no bars in Washington, we drove across the city line to Baltimore and found a sleazy kind of roadhouse. All three of us were quite familiar with sleazy roadhouses and felt not the slightest bit uncomfortable taking a shiny and slightly dirty Formica table and ordering martinis all around. That's what you drank at five o'clock. Some people might order an old-fashioned. Or a Rob Roy. But these we considered too Ivy League and sort of old hat. The margarita was unknown. And if Fred or I ordered that West Coast favorite, the grasshopper, we knew the bartender would only stare at us.

After downing two martinis apiece we set off for Annapolis, where we were going to visit a distant cousin of mine, Fatty Phil Downer. Fred knew him slightly from San Diego, where Phil had been stationed too.

For some reason Phil had decided to stay in the navy and teach at Annapolis. After dinner we sat around the living room of their uncomfortable little house and chatted. There was a lot of that then. I usually sat on the floor to add an informal note.

I noticed Phil sizing up his guests. He was obviously trying to decide what the relationship was among these three people. For the first time I had the sense that perhaps he was drawing the conclusion that something was up between Fred and me since Marion was clearly not of romantic interest to either of us. I noted this but I don't remember being disturbed by it. Perhaps Phil had learned more while sashaying about the Orient in the navy than I was giving him credit for.

We went back to our guest house, deep in the hot night of Washington. Fred and I went promptly to sleep, but in the very early hours when dawn was just creeping through the battered ivory window shades, we were in each other's arms and his body was moving rhythmically on top of mine. When he came out of deep sleep Fred had few concerns about what family and friends might think of him fucking me. He liked to and he did.

We dropped back off to sleep afterward and when we got up to get dressed and be off back to New York, there was no word about it. He didn't seem miffed that I had once again lured him into carnal congress. Maybe being sandwiched in between two sleeping periods allowed him to just hang it up as a nocturnal excursion to be forgotten.

Of all the men with whom I've made love, and they haven't been legion, Fred was the most affectionate. He had a big, soft, loving nature that went with his big, soft, loving body. It was easy to love him. And perhaps undervalue him.

We arrived back at our garage in the Bronx in the late afternoon and went southward on the subway. Marion left us on the Upper West Side, where she shared an apartment with a small, amusing dark girl who was soon to be married.

Fred and I got off the subway in Sheridan Square and walked through the dusk to our little covey of rooms, deep in the leafy courtyard.

Now I wonder why we didn't make love more often than we did. Fred always said that he needed to be aroused by someone else or he would forget about doing it. I don't think he was repressed. Just sluggish. That big body, thick with large, white muscles needed to be given a kickstart from time to time. I wonder if his wife kick starts him from time to time, or if they both have just forgotten about doing it altogether?

Refusing Fred, No. 1

I didn't have sex with Fred only twice when he wanted to. And I regret both times. It was rare for him to initiate sex.

I was coming into the bathroom in that tiny Patchin Place apartment one morning in my pajamas. He was drying off after having taken a bath.

He reached out his arms for me and I was happy to have those big warm arms hold me, even on a muggy New York morning. We began to kiss, which he knew always excited me.

He undid the drawstring to my pajama pants and they fell to the floor. He then started to turn me around so he could enter me from behind. We had made love the evening before and I was still tender.

"I'm too sore," I said and wriggled out of his arms, pulled up my pajama bottoms, and left the bathroom. He turned to the mirror and began to prepare to shave. Fred was easily dissuaded from sex, which makes me even more regretful. I wish now that I had given him all the pleasure I was capable of giving.

Back in Patchin Place

Fred was sitting in the black canvas butterfly chair. He had just come in from his job and was looking big and tired in his cotton suit and striped tie.

He looked at me in an unfriendly way. "What do you really think of me?" he said.

I said, "I think you saved my life." I put down the *New Yorker* I was reading. I was lying on the saggy green daybed in front of the windows. "I don't think I'd kill myself if you left me anymore. But I still feel like the woman in Erich Maria Remarque's *Arch of Triumph*. When you are away from me I feel a whole side of me has been torn away and I'm raw and open and ache a lot."

He stared at me. This was not what he wanted to hear. Why should he? I was talking about myself, not him.

"What do I think about? I don't really think about you. I feel about you. I want to be with you every minute of the day. I want you to stay with me for the rest of my life. I think you're the handsomest man in the world."

"You're not after me to sleep with you as much as you used to be," he said. What was going on in his mind?

"About half the times we do, you tell me you hate me afterward. That's not very encouraging." I was not going to go over there and kneel in front of him and put my arms around him. Not yet. "Look, when this summer is over you're going to go home, you're going back to college. I'm going to have to somehow get along all by myself."

Through the window that gave onto the tiny courtyard I could smell that New York summer smell. The exhaust of cars mixed with the green leaves of the trees in the court and the edge of old brick and cement. Our young bodies encased in cotton from Brooks Brothers, our soap, our skin made us seem young and fresh in this hot, worn, tired city.

I couldn't stand up and take my clothes off and say, "Look, why don't you come into the bedroom and fuck me until my brains rattle?" I didn't know how to do that yet. He would have been shocked and I couldn't be that shocking.

Instead I got up off the daybed and said, "Why don't you go take a shower and I'll make some supper? I'll make that tuna thing over noodles."

"The inexhaustible noodle locker," he said as I passed his chair and reached up and took my hand. I didn't really know how to mother him and expected him to father me. I couldn't sit in his lap in that stupid butterfly chair.

"You're it for me," I said, looking down at his full face, the full lips, the bright blue eyes, the tight blond curls cut short on top of his head. "I don't want to be with anyone else. Like in the Billie Holiday song, 'If that isn't love it'll just have to do until the real thing comes along.'"

He followed me into the tiny kitchen with its little blue flowers all over the walls like wallpaper. He put his arms about me quite gently. He was always more affectionate in that little kitchen because no one could see us in there from any window or doorway. "You're always able to open your mouth and say things you feel, aren't you?" he said.

I pulled back and looked at him. "I don't say anything I don't mean," I said. "I'm going to be sunk when you leave." And pushed him toward the bathroom with the tub that ran downhill.

My Second Lover

Let me digress a bit. My second lover was nothing at all like Fred. Physically somewhat, in that he was tall and blondish. But he didn't like to have his nipples sucked, which Fred loved.

There would be something very interesting to learn about oneself in simply recording your sexual history in detail, leaving your lovers faceless and nameless, only describing their bodies and what they liked to do sexually and how you interacted with them. Because you adapt and find your satisfaction in terms of what they enjoy. And some things you loved doing with one lover you forget and never do again with the next. Who has his own little things he likes and doesn't like.

Robin was a dancer. He also had large thighs like Fred, but I didn't really learn that until he had his clothes off. He had beautiful feet with high arches that looked like some kind of sculpture when he pointed his toes. And he had beautiful hands. Later I couldn't really remember what Fred's feet and hands were like.

Robin's body consistency was completely different than Fred's also. Fred must have been carrying the genetic consistency of English ancestors. The solid white flesh, those full muscles, smooth hairless skin.

Robin's family was Scandinavian. Some blood off the steppes had gotten in there somewhere; those high cheekbones and slightly slanted eyes hinted at Tartars sweeping in from the Far East. His muscles were finer and his skin was tawny and very fined grained. And silky. And his body was very flexible. As a teenager he told me that he often went into the bathroom, locked the door, lay down on the floor on his back, and rolled his feet over his head so he could suck his own penis. He said, "If you think it's exciting to have it in someone else's mouth, it's much more to have it in your own." That excitement was always going to be denied me, unfortunately.

I met Robin at the gymnasium, saw his body in the shower, and had some kind of sex shock. Although we slept together for many years, I don't think you could say I was ever in love with him. I think it was more that I was very deeply and long-lastingly in lust with him. I never did *not* feel like sleeping with him, whatever the occasion or whenever he suddenly appeared. He would return from out of town on tour, call me from the airport, and instead of going home come to my apartment. It was always like some kind of special prize. A piñata of my very own. Robin would be somewhere and then suddenly appear, showering me with gifts of his beautiful body and large penis. I was never a size queen, but his equipment was the largest I've ever seen. Fred had a nice penis but I never concentrated on it. It was the overall making love with a man I loved that was the essence of our relationship.

Robin was something else. He was all about sex. He really did not like to kiss. In fact he was a poor kisser. And when I first knew him did not ever offer to suck a penis in return for his being sucked. Nor did he want anything to do with anal intercourse. Unless it was somebody else's anus. He said, "I really like that as long as I can be sure I'm not hurting them." He was a gentleman, Robin. Which is not something you stumble across in the world of dance very often.

Robin's dance career was doomed by two things. One, he lived on a twenty-six-hour daily cycle that resulted in his going to bed two hours later every day. It was hell to live with him, as some days he was living quite normally and some days he was up all night and slept all day. I was more sensitive in those days and found it difficult to sleep with someone moving about the apartment. Of course, going to class on a regular schedule was impossible for him.

His other failing was the fact that his magnificent body couldn't dance. It could take all positions, and he looked wonderful in photographs. But when the music played he couldn't let go and dance. In class he marked positions and gestured with his hands where he was supposed to go, but in the numerous times that I observed him in class I never really saw anything that could be called dance movement.

One on one Robin could be great. He liked sudden and fanciful decisions to take the subway to Far Rockaway in the dead of night and walk upon the beach at dawn. And he could be funny. Once when I drew a tub of water for him I heard him laughing and he had gotten into the tub fully clothed. There was whimsy there, but a kind of Scandinavian whimsy.

What can we say about people we love? Each one is somehow different. Robin's appeal for me was not romantic. It was sexual. When we first began our relationship, I tried to cast him in the same mold as Fred. A romantic lover who would hold me in his arms and feel affection. This was not for Robin. Affection only embarrassed him. Fucking didn't. And he was always profoundly exciting to me. Where I used to cry out in the night to Fred, "Don't leave me," it was because I couldn't bear being alone. I never cried out "Don't leave me" to Robin. He would only have laughed and thought it was inappropriate for someone of my sophistication. But if I had, it would have been because I couldn't bear the idea of not sleeping with him. I hadn't become what was called a "fuck freak," except for him.

I have always been fun at parties, and one evening at a friend's house I was my usual self, rattling on about literature or destiny or one of the many subjects I was facile about. Robin sat nearby, not joining in. As we walked back to our apartment he broke his silence to say angrily, "It's not fair. People listen to you and they think that you're the one with the brains. Instead of me." Actually I think he was right.

Our life as a couple ended when I agreed to partner a debutante at some stupid waltz ball. Each girl made her entrance with a young man and then waltzed around the ballroom while the other guests applauded. I could always dance well socially, and the sister of a friend at work needed a partner who could waltz. So I agreed to do it. I had my black tuxedo from college. Why not? Robin attended the ball, escorting the girl's mother, who was a widow. We went to one of those tux rental places and got him outfitted. I thought it would be fun for him and it was going to fit into his schedule. He was going to be awake that evening. I figured it out well ahead. Because if he was sleeping there was no waking him up.

He was fuming in the taxi after we dropped the girl—Elsie, Elise? Eleanor?—and her mother off. Once we entered the apartment he went straight to a closet, pulled out a suitcase, and started packing. As he tore off the tuxedo and threw it on the floor he shouted, "That should have been me up there, not you! You're not the dancer!" I had been whiplashed about enough at this point to let him go without a murmur. I just wanted to go to bed. Where Robin went that night I have no idea.

Robin didn't really disappear from my life. We still met and slept together. But that was the end of any plans I had to replace Fred with him. When he came to me years later and wanted us to live together again, as I was the only person who had ever understood him, I could only laugh. But all of this was long after Fred had left my life.

A Trip to Fire Island

Justine was the one who invited Fred and me. Small, birdlike, almost insect-like Justine was a secretary at the advertising agency where I worked. Very black hair, stick legs, large glasses, but still somehow a little chic. She was from Long Island somewhere, perhaps Hicksville, and lived in an apartment in London Terrace with three other girls. We called them "girls" then. You weren't really a woman until you got married and put on too much weight.

The girls were all husband hunting. What else was there for a young woman to do? At the advertising agency there were no jobs for women above the secretarial level, except for a few writers on things like cake mix and lipstick.

So if you wanted to get married you moved into the city and shared a nice apartment with too many other girls. You spent all your money on clothes. And on renting a house on Fire Island with a lot of other girls so you could invite young men out for the weekend.

Justine had a sort of ex- or part-time boyfriend who was also a part-time model. Blond and blue-eyed and kind of handsome. I met him once. He was probably gayish, but what did we know in those days? Being a full-time model sort of said it all, but straight boys could part-time model without anyone looking askance.

Justine was Catholic and I think he was, too. Which would have been perfect if things had worked out. Which was not to be the case. In retrospect I think what the deal was in the case of all these girls, and New York was full of them, was that you captured the attention of some guy, you were very forward, you slept with him (whether you were Catholic or not), and then he felt duty bound to marry you. Young men did that in those days. Sleeping with someone was such a big deal that once a girl had gone "all the way," there was a kind of commitment to follow through by getting married. When I saw Justine with her ex-boyfriend, there was something lingering between them that suggested to me she had put out for him and then he backed out of their little romance. Justine's ploy had not worked and her attention turned itself to me.

Justine was witty and well read, and we laughed and talked a lot in the office. She told me once that I was so neatly dressed that she and the other secretaries had conjectured that my mother picked out my clothes and decided what I should wear to the office. In a later period being so nicely dressed would have told her something. In the 1950s it suggested only that I would be neat around the house and most likely earn a decent living. The ex sold advertising space for a magazine and even I could dope out that he probably wasn't on the road to a real career.

Since I never asked Justine for a date, she proposed that I come out to Fire Island for a weekend. Whether she had met Fred and had invited him, too, or whether I told her I wanted to bring him along, I don't remember now.

One of her roommates, Patty, a pretty gray-haired divorcée, handled feeding the mob who showed up at the house in Ocean Bay Park. Everyone contributed a certain amount of money (ten dollars?) and Patty shopped at the supermarket in town, as the little store in Ocean Bay Park was exorbitantly expensive. How did we get out there? Someone must have driven and taken the groceries in a car. There was a lot of food. I remember that.

We must have taken the train. Got off at Sayville, or more likely Bayshore. Ran like lemmings for the covey of taxis that awaited the train. And fled as though the Russians were coming for the docks. The time between train arrivals and boat departures was brief. So there was a general air of hysteria hovering over the process of "making the boat." Once aboard the boat, the weekend began and everyone fell into a holiday mood. There was much moving around the boat, below decks and above decks and greeting people. This was our first weekend, so we knew no one but Justine and her roommates. But almost everyone else was familiar with one another from having spent a series of weekends together.

What did we wear? We surely must have come straight from work. I can't imagine that we went home and changed. So probably I was in a summer suit with the tie loosened. Once I had decided that I would wear a sport coat and tie to the office on a Friday. I was sent home to change, as only suits were considered adequate office wear.

So I would have been in a suit. Very likely a Haspel cord suit from Brooks Brothers in white with a fine blue line pinstriping it. Or a fine black line. I had both those suits. There was also green and red, but that would have been considered too exotic. Perhaps men in New Orleans, where these seersucker suits originated, might have those, since they wore Haspel suits every day. But in New York it would have been considered flashy. I don't think it would have been considered fruity. No one was really sure what dressing in a fruity way meant exactly, anyway. Everyone was in the same neat uniform and tie and short haircut, which was pretty fruity to begin with. Flashy probably suggested that you might be Jewish, and even if you were it wasn't a look anyone wanted to have in the advertising business. That was for people in the theater or movie business, who wore black suits and white ties on white shirts. Our goal was to look as though we were in banking so as to legitimize the hocus-pocus that was our metier. There was no research then, only force of personality. And clients spent enormous sums of money for work that took a few days to create. Agencies were swimming in dough, and for the advertising executives who held the clients through charm or memberships at the same country clubs the salaries were huge, also. A good hunting ground for girls like Justine and her pals.

I would have been carrying a small bag in which there would be modest swimming trunks, which would well cover all my lower torso. They too might have been made of madras, the fashion breakthrough for men that summer. There would have been no T-shirts, and I think I was still wearing my baggy navy underpants. A pair of Bermuda shorts and a short-sleeved shirt or two. Maybe a V-neck sweater in navy blue. Perhaps cashmere. My steady perusal of the counters at Brooks Brothers had elevated my tastes. My Brooks Brothers charge was so high that one time they called me in to discuss it. I was outraged. I said to them, "How many customers do you have that spend this kind of money? Why do you bother me with this?" They backed right off and let me pay as I could. Fred was always a little astounded at the way I spent money, although he was never asked for a loan.

Once we disembarked on the Ocean Bay Park pier, all our belongings and food were piled into a child's wagon and we trundled along a boardwalk to the little house near the ocean that Justine and her friends had rented. It was a frame house with two bedrooms, a living room, and a kitchen. It was almost bereft of furniture. There was a table and some chairs and a broken-down couch in the living room. The bedrooms each had a double bed with a few weary blankets. That was pretty much it. There may have been a very shabby rag rug in the living room. And nothing was very clean. I think we all immediately put on our bathing suits and ran to the beach to have a swim before the sun set.

Friday evening we helped poor, put-upon, gray-haired Patty prepare a large meal for the many people who materialized for dinner. Mostly men. Many of whom seemed to have no real place to stay. They carried blankets with them and were prepared to spend the weekend nights on the beach. The girls were good sports and served up whatever had been prepared: chili con carne, a large salad, ice cream. That would have been the kind of dinner for many people that was prepared then.

Fred and I had taken the bedroom at the rear of the house. I probably had appropriated it, seeing the tide of humanity that was surging through the house. The girls (were there three or four of them?) all slept on the one bed in the other bedroom. That first night Fred and I were alone in the bedroom and fell asleep early, begging off when the others went trundling off to a bar somewhere.

The next day was spent lying on towels on the sand at the foot of the boardwalk. The style was to cluster all the towels together so everyone was lying side by side, while empty beach reached off in all directions.

Ocean Bay Park was next door to the much fancier Point O'Woods, which was actually separated by a tall wire fence, so Ocean Bay Parkers could not wander over casually. From Point O'Woods to the east there lay nothing but dunes, an ancient miniature forest, and the homosexual town of Cherry Grove. No one we knew had ever been there and there was little discussion of it. It was simply a world we knew nothing about. Beside it the town of Fire Island Pines was being built, but there were still only a few houses and the boardwalks were just being put in place. Its future as a gay summer citadel could not have been foretold.

Beyond that was the tiny town of Water Island and then the very distant town of Davis Park that did not have electricity. No one we knew ventured that far, although there were beach taxis running back and forth with great regularity all day and all night.

Fred and I walked both to the east and the west during the day. To the west the beaches became increasingly full of people, as these were where the earliest settled beach towns stood. They were family towns and there were many children on the beach.

In the afternoon when we walked to the east there was no one. All the young people at Ocean Bay Park remained huddled on their towels and blankets. The whole point of going to Fire Island was for the girls to meet men and the men to get lucky. Exploring the beach held no interest.

I walked the beach with my eyes down, collecting beach glass. Little morsels of worn pale green and blue glass. And sometimes a rich blue from a Pepto-Bismol bottle. And very, very rarely a fragment of red. From the brake lights of some car that had been thrown into the ocean?

Fred rarely quibbled about what I decided we would do. Was that because he was willing to let me make decisions, genuinely liked doing what I wanted to do, or because soon he knew he would be leaving me and saw no reason to argue? He was a kindly person. There was something monolithic about him. Slow to speak. Slow to flare up. A large force that was not easily dislodged from his path, but seeing only the large essentials. The peripheral activities, which were largely what I was interested in, made little difference to him, and he was willing to acquiesce on these activities like taking walks. They were largely irrelevant to him. He fucked in a monolithic way also. When he was moved sexually he was not deterred.

That evening, after another one of our communal dinners, Justine wanted me to take a walk with her in the moonlight. We stood on the wooden deck and looked across the ocean, where the waves were catching the silvery light and the sky was a pale whitish blue. She asked me to kiss her and I did. "You can do better than that," she said.

I said, "Gee, Justine, I don't think I can." And we went back inside.

There were even more revelers in the house on Saturday evening than the night before. Fred and I withdrew to our bed with little notice being paid. Rolled up in the grungy blankets, we went to sleep while the noise of people laughing, glasses clinking, bottles being opened went on around us. Inside and outside the house.

In the night a man who was trying to get into the bed with us awakened me. He sat on the edge of the bed and tried to push me over with his butt. "Aw, c'mon. Make room," he said. I remained immovable. Fred was completely inert beside me. The man said, "Selfish." And pulling his blanket about him left the room.

He must have come back, because when I awoke in the deep black of a night that was not silent, his body in its blanket lay on the other side of Fred. Fred in his sleep had his arms about me and one leg over me.

I turned and pulled him on top of me. I reached down and felt between his legs. He was hard. He put his mouth on mine. He was awake and wasn't going to tell me the next day that I had let him fuck me in his sleep. He placed himself between my legs and began his rhythmic and slow movements. It would have been entirely within reason for the man next to us to have sat up astonishedly and cried out, "Are you two guys fucking?" We would have been thrown out of the house by our horrified hostesses and had to sit on the dock waiting for the first boat out in the morning.

He may have heard or felt us as the mattress surged with Fred's heavy movements. But he did nothing. Half asleep as I was, I found it easy to assume that someone could sleep through two men making love about one foot away. Fred held me tightly as he came powerfully. I let it sink into the mattress. What was I supposed to clean up with? I just went back to sleep sticky. I was already pretty sticky and stinky from salt water and not having been able to get into the single shower.

The morning light blazed through the unshaded windows when I got up, leaving Fred and the stranger on the bed. The living room looked as though there had been an enemy attack in the night. Stray men were lying about the floor and the couch. Across the doorway in the foyer lay one body, warmly enough dressed but without a blanket. There had been some heavy drinking here the night before. Perhaps the stranger in the bed had heard nothing if these snoring, sodden guests sprawled everywhere were an example.

We returned to the beach, lay in the sun broiling all day as we had the day before. Told jokes, ran in and out of the water, looked for beach glass along the water's edge. Probably walked down to the pier at midday to the snack stand to have a hamburger. And at the end of the afternoon took a boat back across the bay and repeated the rush upon the taxis to make sure we made the train.

The train, originating at the far end of Long Island, would have been packed with sandy, reddish, wrinkled folks returning to the sanity and neatness of lives in New York. It *was* saner and neater then. We had no idea that soon there would be so many options about the kind of work we could do, where we could live, and with whom we could sleep.

From Penn Station, which was still the great marble temple under a vast glass ceiling in those days, Fred and I caught a subway down to Sheridan Square and walked under the tired, green trees back to our little apartment. I somehow thought he would be in my life forever, even though I knew he was going back to school in Kansas at the end of summer.

I really didn't realize that the reason I felt my life was going somewhere was Fred.

A Trip to New England

My friend Howard once said to me, "Your only real talent is the ability to act." By that he didn't mean in the theater, but the ability to actually "do." Perhaps he was right. Perhaps I have done too much.

During that New York summer, I always had a plan for Fred and me to do something each weekend. We had our little gray-blue car stashed away in the Bronx, and I, having spent my youth reading in Illinois, knew of many places I wanted to see.

I had long wished to see the world of Maxfield Parrish as he saw it from his studio in Vermont. Those precise mountains and hills, the sun making sharp shadows, the brilliant blue sky carrying masses of carefully arranged clouds. The romance of light on landscape. My mother had always called my attention to the skies and particularly those brief moments during sunset when above there is pink and blue glory that should last forever, but changes after a few moments.

That was the New England I wanted to see and dragged poor Fred after me pell mell to see it.

We must have made rendezvous in Patchin Place about five-thirty. Changed our clothes, packed small bags, and took the subway to the Bronx. Using the express train it was actually quite a rapid trip, and we must have been on the road heading north well before seven. How far could we have gotten before nightfall? I knew that we didn't know exactly where we were going, but we set out to see where adventure might take us. We were perfectly game to spend the night in some down-at-the-heels tourist court.

No one had weekend homes in Vermont or New Hampshire then. There were no great sweeping highways to get a driver there quickly. Two hours out of New York there were still plenty of places that were untrammeled: Bucks County, the Berkshires, the Hamptons. Although people didn't swarm to the Hamptons as they do now. It was more where you went for a long summer vacation. Our weekend clothes were the usual for the 1950s. No T-shirts. No jeans. We wore cotton pants or shorts. With little short-sleeved shirts. White and small plaids. A V-neck sweater in navy blue or maroon. Occasionally in dark green. Yellow, pink, light blue, and red did not exist at Brooks Brothers in sweaters for men.

What did we wear for shoes? Although the loafer had been around for some time it was not generally worn, and certainly not without socks, which became popular later. We wore plain brown shoes with sports clothes. White sweat socks could be worn with them if you were wearing chinos. If you were wearing chino shorts you probably wore Top-Siders with them. The Top-Sider was usually in navy blue canvas with a funny kind of squeegee sole that was supposed to cling to ship's decks. They were worn only when water was in some propinquity; on Fire Island, the Hamptons, the Connecticut shore. I don't think Fred ever owned a pair. He would have looked askance at them as being effete. And I certainly wouldn't have worn them on a trip to Vermont. They were definitely not country wear.

We both probably brought a Haspel jacket in seersucker to wear if we ate in a restaurant. Although a tie wouldn't be necessary in the country.

Wherever we stopped the first night out on our New England trip must have been unmemorable. I have no memory of it. It probably was somewhere in western Massachusetts, in a countryside that rolls increasingly in preparation for the mountains beyond.

My clearest memory is driving in the light of the setting sun through a Vermont village I had already imagined, in the center a village green that was intensely green. Set around the green were white houses. All of them white. With green shutters, some pillared and some not. Larger trees circled the green, making a shady barrier between the houses and the open space they all faced. Golden light flooded between the houses on the side toward the sunset, making the green of the grass and leaves intensely sharp and the white of the houses equally bright and clear. Everything looked as if it had very recently been painted, which it probably had. There must have been side streets and shops somewhere. But I remember only this space filled with green and white and gold, edged in the black of tree trunks and branches and shadows.

We stayed the night in a large white rambling summer hotel, not on the green. The hotel recommended that we eat dinner at another hotel nearby, which we did in our chinos, Haspel jackets, and shirts neatly turned out over the collar.

There was a summer art school of some kind in this village, as there is in most of the villages of Vermont. The two women at a nearby table were discussing an art appreciation course, which they were evidently not finding easy.

Fred excused himself to go to the bathroom. While he was gone one of the women, dark haired and wearing horn-rimmed glasses, said, "When he puts those slides on the wall I just can't tell the difference between Monet and . . ."

"Manet?" her friend suggested, a plumper lady with faded blonde hair who seemed to be enduring the company of her acquaintance more than she was enjoying it.

"Exactly. I try to remember the details, but the more I look at the pictures the more impossible it gets. Monet looks exactly the same as . . ." She searched for the name.

"Manet?" her friend suggested a second time.

"Yes. That's it. So I've just about given up. I don't think I'll ever be able to tell the difference between Monet and . . . and . . ."

"Manet?" the blonde friend inquired for the third time. Still patient and kind.

"Well, you see what I mean!" the horned-rimmed lady said.

They finished their coffee and left just as Fred returned to the table. I had been delighted with their exchange and told Fred, playing the roles of the calm blonde lady and the exasperated art student.

Fred looked at me intently without smiling as I told the story. When I finished, he said, "Was she wearing horn rims and a pink dress?"

I said, "Yes, how do you know?"

"She's sitting right behind you," he said.

I turned. My back had been to some columns that separated the dining rooms from the hotel lobby. The horn-rimmed lady and her friend had seated themselves in wicker chairs only a few feet behind me when they left the dining room. The horn rims were glaring at me close enough to reach out and slap me.

I turned back horrified. Fred was smiling slightly. "You pay the bill," I said and got up and ran out of the hotel.

He emerged in a few minutes and sauntered down the broad front steps. I was waiting under a nearby tree. Once he reached me we burst into howls of laughter as we walked under the dark trees back through the night to our rambling wooden hotel.

Everything in Fred moved slowly and deeply. Even his humor. I liked that about him. It was so unlike myself.

It amused me a lot that he had sat quietly and let me make a complete fool of myself. Being deeply embarrassed in public actually bothered him a lot less than it did me.

In the morning we engaged in some acrobatic sex before we got up. In his own slow-moving way he seemed willing to allow me to explore sexual possibilities, as though he was indulging me by doing things that were of no great interest to him. We wound up with my face between his legs, his cock in my mouth. I was pressing against his ample chest, my butt in his face. He pressed down on my lower spine with both hands as I humped his chest until we both came.

Lying with my head toward the foot of the bed, I watched him pull himself up and go to the bathroom. Through the open door I saw him sit large-muscled and magnificent on the toilet and pull paper off the roll to mop my semen off his chest. Then he stuffed the paper down between his legs and flushed.

I didn't like the feeling that he was allowing us to have sex together with no real enthusiasm on his part. It placed me in an unflattering light, but not so unflattering that I was willing to stop having sex with my great big guy.

Curious, no? If he really hadn't wanted to make bamboola with another man, he could have dropped me before we ever went to New York. But he wanted to do that. Perhaps he pardoned himself by believing that I made him do it. Or that he was doing it for me. If he was just doing it for me, God bless him.

We rolled back down the golden hills toward the end of the day on Sunday, after visiting Norman Rockwell's home in a tiny village deep in a gorge. I thought it strange that so famous a person would want to live in so isolated a place.

Before the day ended, we tucked the little car into its row of garages and climbed the stairs to the subway station that perched high in the air in the Bronx. We climbed out again in Sheridan Square, back in the heat and noise and grassy/gassy smell that had become New York for us.

The Trip to Connecticut with Friends

One of the people Fred and I saw most frequently in New York was my friend Bert. Bert and I had been naval officers together, becoming friends when we met at cryptographic training school.

Bert was a New Yorker born and bred and after leaving the navy had joined his father's plastics business. He had a younger brother named Ned who also worked in the business. Bert was dark and hand-some-like but not at all appealing to me. Ned was blond and taller and I did rather fancy him, in no very serious way.

Bert had met a nurse while he was in a navy hospital for something or other. Was it dengue fever or something equally obscure? As I came to know Bert better, I found that obscure illness was one of his trademarks.

Bert had married the blonde nurse in San Francisco before return-ing to New York, and they were living in London Terrace, that vast brick block of flats on the far West Side on Twenty-Third Street.

When Fred and I first came to New York, Bert and—was it Eloise?—were busily installing themselves in their largish flat. It was much nicer than anything I was used to living in. Wall-to-wall car-peting, upholstered and slipcovered furniture, English antiques. I was used to my family home, in which everything was some ancient non-descript antique handed down through the family, including the beds. Like the story of the Boston women who were asked where they got their hats. Their reply was, "Oh, but we *have* our hats." We al-ready *had* our décor in Illinois.

Of course there was the grandeur of my uncle and aunt's enormous apartment. But that was museumlike. One didn't really *live* there. One stayed there.

So I admired Bert and Eloise's apartment. I saw nothing amiss in their marriage. We had other navy friends living in or passing through New York, and they were all married. All of them seemed to have seized upon some young woman as soon as their navy duty was over. I assumed that heterosexuals knew something I didn't know about finding the right one with whom they could stay forever. I assumed their feelings must be something like what I felt for Fred, but with that extra touch of church and legitimacy thrown in.

When Bert told me later, "When we got done refinishing the furniture we really had nothing to say to each other," I began to realize there was more to it than that. Eloise was ladylike and pretty and had very large bosoms. Bert, I suppose, wanted a wife that other men would envy him for. And he got her. What Eloise had in mind I cannot imagine.

We saw Bert and Eloise regularly for parties and movies and dinner. Bert and I always laughed and talked a lot, and Fred liked Bert. Eloise was always something of the silent partner.

As the summer progressed, a trip into Connecticut was planned with Bert and Eloise accompanying us. Were we planning to go to Tanglewood? Mystic Seaport didn't exist yet. There was certainly some reason or destination. And so we set out. Bert and Eloise accompanied us on the subway to the Bronx, picking up the little car and setting out.

It was late summer with the sun in the mellower mode it gets in August. The countryside was green but a little limper than it had been in June and July. September was hovering and the leaves were yearning to turn and drop.

I'm sure we had a pleasant time. If someone had overheard us I'm sure the conversation could have been lumped under "inane chatter." My brother's always accused me of being guilty of chattering inanely, little realizing what a great social skill it is. Inane chatter was very 1950s. We knew nothing of understanding ourselves and would have had a horror of doing so.

Social interchange was all about being amusing and looking right. I had already mastered that long before I arrived in New York. And it was certainly Bert's social goal. So we had fun, never asking ourselves what was going on in the lives of the people about us. I would guess that in Connecticut the woods are full of folks still living exactly those kinds of lives. With some drugs thrown in.

On Saturday evening we were in some lost place like East Haddam and found some kind of court or cottage establishment. The cottage we took had two bedrooms separated with a wall that ended at eight feet in height. From there up into the peaked roof was empty space. Every shoe dropped or bedspring squeaked could be clearly heard from room to room. Except for the light wall of lath, it *was* one big room. The beds on either side had their heads together, only the thin wall separating them.

Fred and I didn't sleep in the same bed in Patchin Place, so we never had the opportunity to run across each other in the night. We did in this rattletrap of a tourist court cottage, and in the darkness Fred was on top of me, moving himself in and out between my tightly held thighs. I think we were both half asleep with no thought of squeaking springs or panting and gasping.

Shortly after breakfast, Bert announced that Eloise wasn't feeling well and that they were going to have to catch a train back to New York right away from nearby New London or wherever the hell we were.

Incredibly, I did not connect this to the fact that Fred and I made love in the night in that reverberating partitioned room. It just never occurred to me. Or I didn't want it to occur to me. I was very solicitous of Eloise. I imagined that her period had started and I knew that for some women it was very painful and sick making.

What I have also surmised in the years since is that poor Eloise not only had to listen to two men fucking in the next room, but her husband was lying next to her and hadn't the least, or certainly not much, interest in doing the same to her. I'd like to imagine that Bert was lying next to her, not speaking but pretending to be asleep as she was, and wishing he was either under Fred or on top of me. I wonder, I wonder, I wonder.

Once we put Bert and Eloise on the train, we set out in our little blue-gray car to return to New York. Down through that litany of towns: Fairfield, Greenwich, Stamford, and on and on and on.

Fred was furious because he'd fucked me in the night. He didn't say that he thought that was why Eloise was sick. More likely having a heterosexual couple in such propinquity only made the deed more aberrant to him.

"I hate you," he said. "And I hate doing things like that with you. I should just pack when we get back to New York and go home, although I'm not going to because I promised to work all summer. But I'd like to."

Even as I write this I feel some kind of shame, but not much. Whatever shame I felt at his attack was overridden by my determination to keep him fucking me just as long as I had him with me.

I had never had a true lover like Fred and a true love affair. I believed that Fred was being honest and that he really did hate me and hated sleeping with me. At that moment. But I also knew he was capable of drawing me to him and wanting to have sex. That I was not continuously provoking him to sin. Although I don't think it was the sin side of it that bothered him so much.

Once back in New York we continued to see Bert and Eloise socially, and there was no indication on the part of either one that they felt differently about Fred and me. Perhaps I have fantasized much of the episode, and they didn't hear anything on the other side of the flimsy partition.

But before the end of August Eloise announced that she had to go home to San Francisco to visit her ailing mother. Fred and I accompanied Bert in his station wagon when he took Eloise to the airport—La Guardia, which was still a row of Quonset huts near Long Island Sound. Kennedy Airport was called Idlewild in those days and flights rarely left from there. I did note that Eloise seemed to have an awful lot of luggage for someone who was just visiting her mother but attributed it to the fact that women liked to change their clothes a lot.

The next day Bert called me at the office. He was upset but not hysterical. Eloise had called him as soon as she had arrived in San Francisco. Their marriage was over. She didn't say why particularly. Everyone was so polite in those days. Bert probably wasn't being at all romantic or she didn't like being romantic with him. I did not conjecture then and it's probably unfair to conjecture now.

Bert said, "I knew something was wrong when I got home and the silverware was gone." Doesn't that say it all? I can't help but think that hearing Fred jump my bones in the next room led Eloise to decide that it was all over with Bert.

Refusing Fred, No. 2

The second time I denied sex to Fred was more problematical, but even so, I regret it. It was a Sunday morning and we had a house guest in our miniature apartment. Again, I'm not sure how or why we accommodated Barry, a fraternity brother of mine from college who was now in premed at Johns Hopkins. Why was Barry never in the service? Or did he do some kind of medical thing for the armed forces?

It was Fred's turn to be sleeping in the little bedroom. I was on the daybed under the windows. Barry was perhaps on some kind of mattress on the floor.

I woke up while the other two were sleeping. I was probably planning to go to church. I still did that in those days. And wanted to shine my shoes. I took shoes and shine kit into the bedroom, closing the door to avoid disturbing Barry.

I was quiet as I sat on the floor, first rubbing a rag into the can of brown polish and then putting the polish on my Brooks Brothers shoes.

Fred woke and stirred. He turned on his back and partially threw the covers back. He had an erection. He must have glanced at me but kept his eyes shut as he moved his body toward the edge of the bed. He always wore a navy T-shirt and those baggy navy undershorts with the flat front and three buttons in warm weather. I continued to at least wear pajama bottoms topped with a T-shirt when it was really hot.

He pulled the sheets around him so his penis protruded about a foot from me. He pushed his hips back and forth so his penis moved in and out of its sheeting shroud.

I was prudish, even though I knew that Barry on the other side of the door was homosexual, too. Knew in an unspoken way.

What did I think would happen if Barry heard us? That he would throw open the door and shout in a shocked way, "You're sucking his cock!"

Half awake, Fred had dismissed Barry's presence. He wanted sex. He looked through half-opened eyes at me in a pleading way. I nodded toward the door and shook my head. I could lose track of what was important in those days. I probably had the day all planned, and having some secretive sex would throw the schedule off. When we have a partner for sex present, it is easy to dismiss opportunity. Not realizing that the moment of interest and excitement will pass, never to return again.

I should have stood up, stripped off whatever I was wearing, slobbered some spit on Fred's penis, and mounted him as he lay there on that sagging single bed. Sat on his penis with my thighs astraddle his. Let him surge and plunge in and out of me. Leaned forward and kissed him deeply until I pulled a wrenching orgasm out of that large and phlegmatic body. And let Barry hear the pounding and creaking and sighing and groaning through the door. And emerged with shined shoes in my hand as though nothing had happened. I wasn't capable of it then, though I came to be later.

So Fred's hard-on subsided. I finished shining my shoes. And we went off with Barry to the Episcopal Church on Fifth Avenue and Tenth Street. Certainly God wouldn't have minded if I had managed to squeeze in a good screw before church. It was me that minded, and I shouldn't have.

Love in the 1950s

I want to tell you about love in the 1950s. It was different. We hadn't had the 1960s yet. We didn't have rock and roll. We were brought up on songs that suggested that the best part of love was loss. Songs like "I Took a Trip on a Train (and Thought About You)," "The Folks Who Live on the Hill," "I'll Be Seeing You," "Imagination." Love was usually for someone impossible who would never return your love. Or who had once loved you and now had left you behind. Forever.

This was probably a residue of World War II, when men and women were separated and love was very much of the moment. During that time love and sex didn't inevitably lead to marriage and that was probably the wedge that led us to believe and accept that love was temporary, and that led us to even enjoy the pang caused by that temporariness.

At any rate, I always felt that my love for Fred was very fragile. His arms around me, his lips on my face, the warmth of his body in bed, of all these things I always felt keenly aware.

We weren't hard-fucking folk in those days. Any of us. A hand on a penis was already very exciting. A mouth was a very big treat. And anal entry was a kind of commitment. I, being so romantic, felt that Fred should enter me but entertained no thoughts of the reverse.

Once in that tiny bedroom as I was lying on top of Fred, he rolled his hips up so that it would have been easy for me to enter him. But I did not. I was almost shocked that he would consider playing the role of the woman. I was the woman. He was the man. If he became the woman I would have to become the man, and I wasn't ready to do that. The idea that entering would have given him pleasure and it was something he wanted did not occur to me.

Sexuality as sexuality was a 1960s phenomenon. We had never seen Mick Jagger. The culture we lived in was very polarized. Women and men dressed nothing alike. Did nothing alike. Had no jobs alike.

There was no encouragement to cross the sexual barrier. I guess I deserve some credit for not having thought much about it and for having dragged Fred with me willy-nilly. No matter how much he might have felt that I introduced him to forbidden and perverse vices, he enjoyed them. And was frequently a leader and improviser.

But there was nothing excessive or violent or tough about our sex life together. It was veiled, indeed swathed, in the thrill of actually doing these things with someone you loved. The idol, the unattainable one, was actually there and you were both naked and you found orgasm in each other's arms. It was a big deal and not readily available. I valued it and Fred valued it when he was alone with me.

Have I captured any of this for you? Women in full skirts and little waists. Small hats, short curly hair, white gloves, and a purse. Men in dark, single-breasted suits that didn't fit all that well, striped button-down shirts, knit ties, dark shoes, and short hair.

The idea of two men throwing those suits aside and falling into each other's arms was something few could imagine. And when it happened you felt that you were very rare, isolated, unique. And that your love was unique. That it was a love that really had no place in those suburban homes and shiny cars and kitchen.

Fred had said once early in our romance as he held me in his arms, "I wish I could take you away to a desert island somewhere." In that world, who could be blamed for thinking it was the only solution?

The pull of the image of a curly-haired woman in the full skirt beside the kitchen counter was strong for Fred. I guess I knew it would eventually win out.

One evening when I came home from work Fred told me he wanted to date a girl he had met at his office. "I miss that," he said. I didn't object. How could I?

And I was beginning to flag in my pursuit of Fred. Being the one who almost always initiated sex, being the goad to museum going, theater attending, and nightclub haunting, being the one who found life thrilling. My attention was beginning to wander.

I was beginning to wonder what it would be like to sleep with some man other than Fred. Beginning to want a lover who really wanted to be in love; not one I felt I was dragging into a relationship he would willingly escape.

When Fred came in from his date with the girl from the office, he slumped into the black butterfly chair and seemed chagrined. Whoever she was, she had been disappointing. And here he was, stuck again in our tiny apartment with me.

Death in the 1990s

The last time I saw Marion Padwee, she was dying. I wasn't sure of it, but it seemed pretty certain. She was the only friend that Fred and I had known in the 1950s whom I still saw.

She had drifted in and out of my life ever since. From her rather old-maidy stance of our youth, she had gone on to marry a number of times. Once to a handsome Frenchman, with whom she had had a child.

Returning to New York, she had become blonde and a sort of girl-about-town, living with her mother and little son on Gramercy Park. I saw quite a lot of her in the 1960s. She told me that a wealthy suitor had given her a pearl necklace and that her mother had immediately taken it to a jeweler the next morning for appraisal. If it was real and valuable it meant the suitor was going to ask her to marry him. "Men never give really valuable jewels unless they are planning to marry you and get them back," she said.

She eventually planned to remarry her French husband but met another man on the flight back to France, changed planes at Orly, and went on to Mexico with him. She was married to him for a number of years. I only learned of the change of plans when I received the Frenchman's wedding announcement and discovered that the bride's name wasn't hers. The French husband evidently had a backup in mind whom he promptly married when Marion did a bunk on him.

What happened to the second husband was always unclear to me, but Marion eventually married a man whom she referred to as "the condom king of New Jersey." I only met him once at dinner. He was large and handsome and reminded me a little bit of Fred. I wondered if Marion had been attracted to Fred in those long-ago days. She had never seemed to be.

The condom king seemed very eager to please Marion, whose manner had an edge of disdain. They were about to move to London, where condoms were calling, evidently.

I thought he was quite a catch actually, but Marion had reasons for not being happily married. What they were I was never told. But at lunch some years later she said, "Next week is my birthday and for a present I'm going to give myself a little divorce." I didn't want to get into it.

I had recently come to theorize that homosexuals acted the way women would if they were free from the possibility of childbirth and the difficulty of economic survival. Marion was proving my point. When she got bored with a man she was on to the next one.

Then AIDS struck, the condom king became far richer than he had ever dreamed of being, and Marion decided not to quit him. He probably bought her out. And perhaps that decision was the fatal one.

The last time I saw Marion, we had lunch at Bice. She had recently had a lot of chemotherapy and made no bones about it. She was very thin but no thinner than most of the women in the restaurant. Her shoulder-length blonde hair was clearly not her own, as it had far too much shine and body for someone of her age. But she looked chic. And she was fun. But I sensed that she was fading.

It was like bidding adieu to the 1950s, that farewell lunch with Marion. She sat straight, asked quarter from no one, and made no explanations. And what was going on in her private life was nobody's business but her own. There were no queasy self-explorations or trying to get close to me. She had never asked any questions about my own private life and wasn't about to start now.

As we ate dessert, a mixture of wild strawberries and cultivated garden ones with crème fraîche for both of us, I asked Marion, "Do you remember Fred?"

"Jorgensen?" she said.

"Yes. I'm surprised you remembered his last name," I said.

"I remember him very well. He was very sweet. And in his own soap-and-water way he was very sexy."

"I was so crazy about him," I told her.

"I know. Of course in those days we never talked about it. Or knew quite what was going on. But you used to look at him with those big calf eyes of yours. Mooning, I think you could call it. Actually, he was something to moon over. What ever happened to all those big, blond guys? You never see them around anymore."

"Your husband is sort of that type."

"Not really. Fred was a very nice guy."

"Your husband isn't?"

"Yes. But not intelligent. I remember Fred being a lot of fun. Remember when he said my hair was perfectly fine?"

We both laughed and for a moment we were back in that car in Washington, the hot summer air blowing in. It seemed a very long time ago.

"Do you still stay in touch with him?" Marion asked. "I hope he's happy somewhere."

"I think he is," I said. "He married. He had three children. He's a successful lawyer. All the things he wanted."

"It was very clear that he was heading for that. You always pick the buds that aren't going to blossom for you, don't you, Bill?" Marion still always called me Bill because we had been in school together when everyone called me that.

"He had a kind of magic when I first knew him. But he wasn't really interested in his own magic," I said.

"Maybe all the magic he had bloomed when he was with you. Maybe that was the blossom. Maybe the wife and kids just got the big, solid plant," Marion said. "I hope you slept with him."

"I did. A lot. He was the only really decent man I've ever been with," I said.

"Well, a man doesn't have to be decent to be great in bed. He doesn't even have to be sane. I'm here to be a witness to that," Marion said and we laughed and laughed some more.

"Don't be sad about Fred," Marion said. "We both have had a lot to learn in life. You couldn't have learned what you needed to know from Fred. And he probably learned all he needed to know from you before he left. Besides, my darling, it's all over. It's in our deep, dark past. When there's nothing to be done about it, let's not waste a moment's emotion. It's over." And with that she started talking about her friend Judy Collins, the singer, whom she was meeting for drinks at the end of the afternoon.

As we left the restaurant she walked ahead of me, slender and straight in ash-blue. She was going to her doom, but she was going with dignity and not making it harder for anyone else. We were both survivors from the 1950s. My strong feelings of attachment for Marion were like those of people who have crossed the great American desert and lived to tell about it. We were both still alive, like those who survived the *Titanic* or the *Hindenberg*. And we shared that essential New York feeling—we didn't really care what our lives were like as long as other people envied us.

And I think that they did, two tall, well-put-together, faired-haired people passing self-assuredly into the street. We must have enviable lives somewhere. How could we not have?

So we parted, Marion to die—I can only hope that when my turn comes I will die as well—and I to my life. A life in which God has always given me the very best of my second choices. My first choices I have never been asked to keep. At least not yet.

Our Last Night Together

Fred was leaving in two days. He was going back to school in Kansas. He wanted to become a lawyer. I was taking it very calmly. I think I had gathered confidence in my ability to evoke lust in other men. I had clung to Fred because, as many young people do, I couldn't believe anyone else would ever want to make love to me. To my credit I had come to have this assurance. To my discredit I was ready to let Fred go. Perhaps if he hadn't always made it very clear he would like to stop making love to me, I might have felt differently.

Two nights before his departure, we went to dinner with Bert. Bert seemed to have quite forgotten his departed wife and insisted on taking us to the Veau d'Or. The Veau d'Or was *the* restaurant in New York in the mid-1950s. Off Lexington Avenue somewhere north of Fifty-Seventh Street, it was a conventional French restaurant with the conventional décor, flowers, gilt, low golden lights to make everyone look good. And the food featured *cervelle* and tripe and all those dishes made of offal that no American restaurant would dream of serving. I had been there before and was in no way intimidated. I took to glamour like a fish takes to water, and Fred always came swimming right after me. Figuring if I wasn't impressed, he wasn't going to be.

We drank a lot of wine and laughed a lot and had the kind of evening that Bert and I specialized in. Amusing conversation about nothing much at all. Fred had become quite good about adding his own deadpan observations. As one of my clients, Charles Revson, said later about advertising, "You can be funny but don't be witty." Bert and I were witty but Fred was really funny. I'm sure his brief tenure in New York stood him well in later years.

As we stood on the sidewalk in front of the Veau d'Or in the warm autumn wind I decided, rather drunkenly, that Fred and I would stay overnight at Bert's in London Terrace. I envisioned the large double bed that Bert had occupied with Eloise and wanted to be in it with

Fred, rather than spilling out of one of the narrow beds in our little apartment.

Everyone fell in with me with no questions asked. Bert slept on the large couch in his living room. How could I have possibly couched this suggestion in a way that didn't confirm for Bert that Fred and I were fucking? Or perhaps Bert knew very well and felt no reason not to cooperate. It is beyond me now, but my suggestion was carried out and within an hour we were in Bert's apartment and lying in each other's arms in the light from the windows with their open curtains. There was no reason to close the curtains on the eighth floor. I had no idea that before very long I would be sleeping in that bed regularly, and seated on that bed that I would hear Fred's final and fatal farewell.

Once in Bert's bed I found I couldn't really give myself over wholeheartedly to making love. Something was holding me back. Perhaps I was unable to forget that Fred was about to leave. Perhaps I had already set my mind on finding someone new. I must have been less than responsive, because to my enormous surprise Fred turned his body around and began sucking me. He had never done that or even indicated that it was a possibility. He was my great big heroic lover and was supposed to smother me with his body. Talk about unsophisticated. But you have to start somewhere.

I pulled his mouth off my cock and drew him to me, kissing him with great fervor. While he was struggling toward his orgasm on top of my body, one part of my mind was expecting Bert to burst through the door and throw the lights on while heaping imprecations upon us as deviants and perverts. I am the furthest thing from paranoid, but this thought distracted me and kept me from giving myself completely to Fred the last time we ever made love. Did I realize that this was the case? I think I did. I didn't seem to care all that much while it was happening. So it goes. We don't care and then we care very much.

In the morning we staggered back to our flat in Patchin Place to change and go to work. Bert was always up early to get to his father's plastics factory before the workers arrived, so we must have made very cursory adieus. Bert and I were going to Fire Island to spend the weekend with Justine and her gang after Fred left early Saturday morning.

The very last evening we had as a house guest Jerry Beaber, who had been in officer's training with me and was going to drive part of the way west with Fred. Jerry was quick and annoying and fast-talking in a way that suggested he felt he was smart and amusing, which he really wasn't. But underneath his glibness I felt a lot of fear, so I was always kind to him. Probably expressing a liking for him that I didn't really feel.

Jerry was from Brooklyn and thought it would be easier if he stayed overnight with us so as to get an early start. I should have been assertive and told him no, but I didn't. Again, it was part of my feeling little regret that Fred was leaving.

He said as much to me in the bathroom while Jerry had run down to the corner for razor blades or something.

"You're really not sorry I'm going, are you?" he said.

This surprised me. I was sure he was happy to be getting away from me. Despite my lack of experience, I knew the right answer.

"I don't really know what I'm going to do," I said. "I'm going to be completely lost, but I'm trying to put a good front on it." I don't know if I delivered these lines convincingly, but I tried.

"You're not crying," he said through the toothpaste in his mouth, looking at me in the mirror.

Looking back at him in the mirror, I felt a quick flash of my old excitement for my curly-headed blond Adonis.

"I will always love you forever," I said. "You will always be the handsomest man in the world for me." And I came up behind him and held him tightly. He put his free hand over my clasped hands that were around his middle, then reached for the glass to rinse out his toothpasty mouth. Little did I know that I was telling the truth.

In the morning the car was quickly packed. When did we bring it down from the Bronx? Maybe we went up the evening before and drove it down. Jerry cracked jokes on the sidewalk in front of Patchin Place. Fred and I didn't kiss or even hug. I wonder if we even shook hands. People didn't, as a matter of course, and I notice in the Midwest they still don't.

And then they were gone. Around the corner and up Sixth Avenue and away to the Holland Tunnel. I had to hurry to meet Bert at Pennsylvania Station and be on our way to Fire Island. The weekend must have been jolly. I have photographs. Me in plaid bathing trunks and a white shirt. Bert hairy chested, both of us on each side of some small, smiling girl. A roommate or friend of Justine's. I do remember that she was more ladylike than the rest of her crowd.

When I walked back down Tenth Street toward Patchin Place at the end of the day on Sunday, warm and sunburned and alone in the loneliness that was then and still is a summer Sunday afternoon in New York, it hit me. I was alone. Fred had really gone. There was the abyss reaching in front of me. Lying on the bed in that empty, still little apartment, the future seemed vast and sad and full of shadows. What was ever going to become of me? I was immediately more in love with Fred than I had ever been before.

A Rainy Night

No matter how long ago something happened, there can be moments when there is an instant connection. Time falls away.

I was in a taxi on Greenwich Avenue in a night rain. We were stopped at a light. In the shelter of a doorway across the street, a dark-haired man in shirtsleeves was holding a younger blond man who was crying in his arms. The younger man, really still almost a boy, was wearing a raincoat.

I immediately created the scenario. The blond boy was in love with the man. Had perhaps slept with him. Had fallen in love and been ignored. Had come through the rain in the night to ring the bell and tell the handsome older man. Who didn't really care but was enough of a gentleman to at least hold him in his arms. And perhaps remember faintly what it felt like to love someone enough to cry about it.

The blond boy looked so much like I had back in the days with Fred. I almost started crying with him. And longed to have Fred's arms about me. The only man, really, who had ever comforted me. All of this in the few seconds before the light changed. The flash took me back to Patchin Place, which was only a few hundred yards away from where the taxi stood on the wet street, the neon reflecting from its shiny black surface.

And then the taxi moved, rushed uptown, away from the blond boy crying in the doorway in his lover's arms. I wished him well. He was going to need it.

The Aftermath

Fred arrived in Kansas safely. I sent him a subscription to *The New Yorker* once he found a shabby room in a rooming house near the University of Kansas. He wrote very regularly in his tiny, tortured handwriting and spoke of his plans to come back to New York the following summer.

I, of course, had quickly abandoned my plans to find a new love and was focused squarely upon Fred again. To fill time, I enrolled in a painting and drawing course at the New School. And moved from the Patchin Place apartment into Bert's apartment in London Terrace. Eloise was definitely not coming back. He never spoke of a divorce, but it was evidently done efficiently and quietly. The only thing he ever said of Eloise subsequently was that she had had breast reduction. I remember her as having large but not enormous breasts. Perhaps she had grown tired of attracting the kind of men who were first drawn to her breasts and then to her personality. She had returned to nursing, that I also knew.

Whatever Bert may have concluded about Fred and me, he proceeded to include me in the carefree whirl of his bachelor life. He had many parties in his Early American apartment, and young women and young men passed through in abundance. It was very much an extension of college life. There were no drugs. Lots of booze and very little scoring. Pre-Pill young women were very careful to trade their bodies for premarital commitment. And the men I knew didn't seem to be terribly keen on getting laid anyway. Of course I knew a better class of young men. These were not blue-collar workers roistering in bars. These were all young lads on their way to the suburbs. How many of them were pregay I have no idea.

Bert and I took turns using the bed and the couch. One week I had the bed and he had the couch; the next week we exchanged.

I believe Bert's real concern in life was to please his blustering father, a fuller, thicker-eyeglassed version of himself. The younger brother resembled Bert's rather good-looking mother.

I laughed a lot when she told me she had been walking down a New York street when a man hailed her from a car. Being very nearsighted, she had to leave the curb and go right up to his car window to see who he was. As she bent down to look in the man said, "Isn't your name Betty?" Once she realized he thought she was a hooker, she quickly regained the sidewalk and didn't know whether she should be miffed or pleased as she mixed back in the crowd. She was quite a good egg but didn't seem to play a very large part in the lives of her sons, who had to please the old man.

The degree to which Bert wanted to please the old man came home to me the morning I fainted in the bathroom. I was standing by the toilet as Bert was shaving. We must have been relatively intimate for me to be peeing with him so nearby. As I fainted he caught me, but the bridge of my nose connected with the sharp edge of the shelf above the toilet. Blood spurted forth in a fountain from the unsuspected vein between my eyes. Bert pressed a washcloth to the cut, got me onto the bed, and called a doctor. And then said he must go as he didn't want to be late for work. The blood was filling the washcloth quite rapidly, so he threw me a towel and said he'd leave the door open so the doctor could get in without my getting up. And left.

The doctor soon arrived and sewed up the cut between my eyes. I remained in bed that day and pondered my basic irrelevance in Bert's life.

Many evenings I called Fred at his rooming house while he was studying. The phone was in the hall and other students would grab it and call up the stairs for him. He was feeling very much alone and very much older than the other students. And he missed New York. The subtext was that he missed me. He wasn't doing well in school. Before joining the navy he had attended a semester of college somewhere and flunked out, so this possibility hung over his head.

After two months the tenor of the phone calls changed. He was getting better grades and had met a young woman who was auditing his freshman zoology class. She already had a degree in mathematics and was working on an advanced degree in preparation for a teaching position at the university.

They hit it off. And more than hit it off, I learned one night as I sat on the big bed in Bert's bedroom. They had fallen in love. Fred was going to marry her.

What a strange feeling. I had been crossing this wide sunlit plain looking forward to my life and Fred's return and some kind of vague future. And suddenly I looked down and there was a deep, black chasm at my feet. The plain stretched ahead but now was far distant. I was stopped dead with a bottomless pit waiting for me to fall into.

I drew back. I told Fred how happy I was for him. He was probably expecting hysterics. I gave him middle-class acceptance.

We continued to have a friendly correspondence after this. I still have the letters. In his tight handwriting with the occasional flourish of a single letter here and there he talked about long rides in the country to talk about their future together. He was very concerned about how he was to pay me for my half of the car. Some 300 dollars. Quite a lot of money in the late 1950s. That was something like a monthly salary for me. I told him my part of the car would be my wedding gift to him.

My evening painting classes were pretty much all I had that interested me. I had advanced from sketching to painting plaster casts. I sent him and his new fiancée one of a female torso and one of a cast of the head of Michelangelo's *The Captive*. Or is it *The Slave?* You know the one. Head thrown back, some kind of cords wrapped around the body. Is he suffering or coming?

I left Bert's strange dead life, the apartment that had once held a marriage, the bed where I made love to Fred rather unsatisfactorily for the last time. There was an apartment available in Patchin Place right upstairs over the one Fred and I had occupied. By midwinter I was back there.

This apartment had a large platform bed in the bedroom. I bought a new foam rubber mattress for it and painted the room pale blue.

The landlord came to look at it.

"Is it all right?" I asked him.

"Rather virginal," the white-haired, bearded old goat said.

"Why not?" I said.

I had picked up a very handsome, rather short young man who worked with me. He was on the edges of New York society and was breaking up with his pretty wife. He stayed with me when things were going particularly badly with the little woman.

He came pounding on the door very drunk on a rainy night. I got up and let him in, and after he had collapsed and passed out on the couch I noticed a letter he had thrown on the table as he came in. It was addressed to me in Fred's handwriting. It must have been on the floor in the lower hall and I had missed it when I came in.

I sat at the table in the chilly, wet night to read it, Billy Pierson mumbling and belching across the room under the blanket I had put over him.

Fred wrote that he no longer wanted to stay in touch with me. "There are some things that a man will never tell his wife and you are one of them," he wrote. Fred could get melodramatic when the occasion warranted it. I looked at Billy Pierson on the couch. Was my life going to be taking in drunks on rainy nights from now on? I felt really sick and went to bed.

Very soon after that I quit my advertising job and enrolled full-time in art school, paying for it with part-time jobs. I really loved painting and so plunged headlong into a life where I could love something that wasn't going to leave me.

My Third Lover

This isn't going to go on forever. I haven't had all that many lovers. Although they seem to be getting shorter and darker. As one of my friends said, "If you keep going on in this direction, you're going to wind up with a pygmy from the African deserts."

Umberto was shorter and darker than Fred and his predecessor Robin. He was a singing-dancing-actor who looked like Tyrone Power. I was ten years older than Umberto and it took me quite a long time to land him. I always get what I want finally, and I've tried to be a good sport about it.

There was a lot about Umberto to be a good sport about. He was the original "step in your own knickers" kind of guy. Is it called "the will to fail"? He was great in summer stock because just about the time he was having fights with the choreographer and infuriating the director, he was on to another show somewhere else.

I kept him on a daytime soap for about a year by getting all my friends all over the country to write fan letters on a weekly basis. I actually got a bunch of teenagers to come to my apartment and write the letters on a large assortment of stationery that I had assembled. Then sent the letters out to be mailed back from Wichita and Spokane. I even sent the teenagers to wait for him at the stage door at the studio where the show was taped. His producers were impressed. And the director had plans for him on Broadway. But that fell through. Probably because Umberto wouldn't sleep with him. I can't imagine why not, as he had slept with half the eastern seaboard by the time our ten years together were over.

I always say that Umberto was the great love of my life. I guess that it's true. He was a great kisser. And one of those guys who feels he's a failure if he doesn't fuck your brains out every time you go to bed. I certainly knew I'd been fucked after a session with Umberto. I loved Umberto in a way that had nothing to do with him as a person. He was self-centered and inattentive, and had been very spoiled by his Italian mother. But once sexually aroused he was quite capable of giving me his full attention. Is that Italian? He was the only Italian I have ever slept with, so I can't be a witness to that.

I learned a lot just dealing with Umberto. At first I was whiplashed back and forth when he failed to show up when he said he would, when he didn't want to sleep with me when I wanted to sleep with him, all the usual crap that sexy young men dish out. But over the ten years I learned to live in terms of many options. If he didn't show up I had a painting I wanted to finish, a book I was reading, a movie I wanted to see. I really didn't care.

At the end of the ten years I realized that although my painting career was gradually doing better and better, Umberto wasn't going to make it in the theater. Every time he was on the brink of doing something important, he would pull the rug out from under himself. And had more and more paranoid ideas about why things weren't working for him. It was always someone else's fault. When I would gently suggest that perhaps there was a pattern to be seen, he would flare up with, "I knew you'd take their side!"

And love wore out. Or perhaps I learned to turn it off. I always felt like sleeping with him. But I saw that the only way we could continue to have a relationship would be to go crazy right along with him. I think some partners do this. The world they share with their lovers is the important one. So they leave the reality of the real world together. I couldn't do that.

As he entered his thirties, work became less and less available to Umberto and he took a job selling ties in a men's shop. He's still there. I see him occasionally. You've heard the adage, "It's better to have loved and lost than to have loved and won?" Umberto is the living example of that one, also. Italian men tend to get smaller and drier as they get older. And crankier. They are all momma's boys. And when momma isn't around anymore and there is no wife to become momma, their lives become one long dissatisfaction. Except for opera. Umberto loves opera and can talk about Renata Tebaldi's *Madame Butterfly* at great length. I'm so glad I'm not there to hear about it.

Umberto has no lover now. I think I was the only long-term one. But no matter how old I get, I'll never go back to him. There wouldn't be any of that masterful fucking. And you can only constantly agree with a man on any subject when he's delivering total satisfaction in the bedroom. Without the sex there's nothing lovable about Umberto. This must be the story of many couples. I'm lucky I escaped.

Whatever Happened to Fred?

So where is Fred now? Do you think I don't know? You don't know me. I know exactly where he is. Fred finished school. Finished law school. And now has his own practice with several partners in Oklahoma City. I can imagine he has made money.

Two years ago on a Sunday afternoon in Paris, I was wondering how many of my lovers were still alive. So I called all of them. It didn't take hours. There never were many. I had always kept track of Fred through his alma mater. I would call the alumni office and they were always able to tell me where he was. The first job in St. Louis. His own law office in St. Louis. Small. The move to Oklahoma City. Was the wife from Oklahoma? Somehow I don't think so. Probably he recognized that his bigger city know-how would stand him well in smaller Oklahoma City. Or perhaps a very major client was easier to handle from there. Fred was always astute.

So I called him. It was early afternoon in Oklahoma, evening in Paris. Do you remember the fragrance? Evening in Paris, I mean. Not Afternoon in Oklahoma. He was very youthful sounding. I thought perhaps it was his son. When I asked if it was him, at first he didn't sound certain. Then I said, "I was thinking of you and wondered if you were alive. So I called to find out."

"I'm alive," he said, almost grudgingly.

I asked him how many children he had. He didn't slam down the phone but told me he had three, two boys and a girl. The two boys were both married and in their thirties. Which was rather young considering Fred's age. But of course he hadn't been able to have children until he had finished law school. The daughter wasn't married. *Not pretty?* I thought. *A lesbian, perhaps?*

Fred had once said to me, "This experience with you will help me understand other people when I'm a lawyer." It's true. He can't be too bigoted about sexual shenanigans, having humped my bones with enthusiasm many a time, whether he chooses to remember it or not.

I suggested that perhaps one day his wife and he might visit me while I was in France. He said, "I don't think that's going to happen." I told him I remained very much the same physically. He said, "I have a little extra weight, but I'm in good health."

I wondered if what he considered a little extra weight would be what I considered fat. His strong, large thighs might have turned into a waddle. I hoped not.

I did not say that I would like to see him again. I did say that I thought of him often. He did not say that he did similarly. He handled me gingerly as we spoke but did not seem to be particularly eager to ring off. And we said good-bye.

So I knew that he was alive. Still married to the same woman. He had his respectable family. Lived in a respectable neighborhood. Did respectable work. His parents and brothers could be proud of him.

The things I really wanted to know were left unasked and unanswered. Did he still sleep with his wife? Did he enjoy it? Did he still get drunk once a week to relax? Did I remain in his memory as an exotic peccadillo, an early romance, a wandering off the path, a falling into the hands of a hysteric who had to be humored? Or was it a dark, ugly thing that he can only pray will never be discovered? I can only hope that his years in law would give him some kind of dispassionate, forgiving, understanding attitude toward himself.

I wonder what his children would think if they knew this chapter in Dad's life. Wouldn't it make a lot of difference to know that your serious, kindly, sort of old-fartish father had once been a handsome young stud slogging it to another guy in the hot, summer nights of a highly charged New York all those many years ago? It would have to create a very different point of view about the old codger. And how many other old codgers are there like Fred out there? Who spent erotic nights in wild places with men who loved returning their grubbing, tongue-hungry kisses. Who opened their thighs wide to receive those handsome young bodies. Why is that anything to be ashamed of? Why is that anything one would want to forget?

Whatever Happened to Me?

What would it have been like if Fred and I had stayed together? Would we have become like those sturdy, full-bodied pairs of white-haired gay men that you see around Provincetown and in San Francisco? Fooling around with younger men but never separating?

Or would we have become increasingly gay, gay, gay as some male couples do? And join some other male couple for heavy-drinking, heavy-laughing dinners where Fred would indicate with both hands in front of him not the length of a fish that he had caught but the length of some cock he had recently sucked or seen or that was lying about. I, of course, would be too thin and smoking a lot and reminding people at the next table of Hedda Hopper. I can only hope that there are some male couples somewhere I might admire. But I've never seen them in public. Maybe they're in Vermont somewhere.

I wouldn't have liked any of those eventualities for Fred and me. I loved him too much for that.

I really had only two major lovers after Fred. And a couple of well-intentioned mistakes. I mistakenly thought at one time that if someone really wanted to sleep with me, there was no harm done in granting him that courtesy. But it was horrible. Like going to the gym. Some people call it a mercy fuck.

So I haven't slept with a lot of people after Fred. But the ones I slept with, I slept with a lot. Hundreds of times. I don't think I could say thousands of times. That's a lot of fucking. But I could say that my attention has always been focused on my private life, even though I've had quite a major success as a painter.

I'm well known. I have my clients. I wouldn't consider myself a society painter, but I do paint really good, solid oils and I don't glue pieces of dishes on them that fall off later.

I love painting and I love Velasquez and Sargent and Goya. And maybe El Greco. I like a large canvas and strong color and painting that is to be viewed from a good ten feet away.

For quite a long time when I was with my second lover I worked as the manager of a restaurant. Lunch only. I waited table some at first but moved up. I had a college degree and I could handle people. I ran into people from my days in advertising who undoubtedly thought I was down on my luck. But I really didn't register that because as soon as I was off work I was in my loft in Coenties Slip painting away.

I never really knew other painters. The whole Jackson Pollock slopping paint around thing passed me by. The Andy Warhol art-making-fun-of-art period kind of got past me, too. I did portraits of people and they liked them and bought them. And they bought my flower paintings, too. And some of my landscapes.

My second lover, the dancer, linked me to the classics. He never really got past about 1930. He disliked Balanchine and only liked dancing with emotion. My painting was about emotion, too. It wasn't painting about painting.

I got a little exhibit way up on Madison Avenue after about ten years and I sold everything. I was very lucky. I was reviewed in the *Times*. I think the reviewer saw more than was there, but he saw me as a modern link to the past and liked it. So the gallery gave me another show. You know, it takes about a year or more to get enough stuff together to make a show. And if you have enough clients you really only have enough painting to go around. It doesn't take a lot of clients to consume as fast as you paint.

My gallery moved. I moved with it. We had windows on the street. Am I famous? I wouldn't say so. Will I live on in the annals of art? I doubt that very much. But who knows? And finally, who cares? No one knew van Gogh while he was living. And although he's world famous now, he's dead. I can't help but believe that the only things that are important are the things you know about.

I've been lucky. I made money. I own a loft. Not the one in Coenties Slip. That's long gone. But another perfectly good one in Tribeca. And I have a little flat in a very unfashionable part of Paris in the Tenth Arrondissement where I go part of every year.

As far as my private life is concerned, I'm not the nice person I once was. I think you can see too much of the world. I learned a lot from my lovers subsequent to Fred. Not that they had any intention of teaching me anything. A longtime friend who knew them both wrote me recently. She said, "They were so chintzy emotionally. As if everything they were, their entire humanity, hung handsomely between their legs."

I've always said, "The good Lord gave me all the best of my second choices." And it's true. All I ever really wanted was to love and be loved by someone like Fred. That was to be denied me. Success in my career, a cultivated and rich life, amusing and interesting and loyal friends, all that I have. But to be honest, none of it is as fulfilling as when Fred was lying on top of me.

Susan Orleans who wrote *The Orchid Thief* said something that struck me forcibly vis-à-vis obsession when she wrote,

> I was starting to believe that the reason it matters to care passionately about something is that it whittles the world down to a more manageable size. It makes the world not huge and empty but full of possibility. If I had been an orchid hunter I wouldn't have seen this place [the backwoods of Florida] as sad-making and vacant—I think I would have seen it as acres of opportunity where the things I loved were waiting to be found.

Painting has given me some of that. But Fred gave me more. He wasn't emotionally chintzy. He made it easy. So I thought it could happen again. And although I have had passion and romance and glamour galore, I never had that feeling of being exactly where I was supposed to be again.

My Fourth Lover

Can I really call Henri Charles my fourth lover? I certainly loved him in the way only homosexuals can. But we never slept together. There was a lot of fondling and a certain amount of fooling around, but we were not lovers. Although a lot of people undoubtedly thought we were.

I had gone to England to live for some years, some inspiration, and some fulfillment of dreams. I was always an Anglophile, out there in the wilds of Illinois. When I was younger it was often said that I resembled the Duke of Windsor, although taller. I never discouraged the comparison. I always admired public figures like Cecil Beaton and Dame Edith Sitwell, although it took awhile for me to figure out the difference.

One of my clients was a very pretty woman—a girl, really, when I met her—from New England who had married a wealthy young banker of some vague South American provenance. He was transferred to London. I visited them briefly there and C. C. said I should move there. She had rapidly assimilated herself into London society and knew a raft of baronesses and ladies and such. So I moved, got a little show at the Hartnell Gallery, and was able to support myself rather nicely.

At my first gallery opening, C. C. introduced me to Henri Charles. Who, despite the rather swell name, was a young American who had come to London for a job assignment with a movie company that had fallen through. He was living temporarily with friends of friends and wanted desperately to stay in London.

Henri Charles was what could be called by many a hunk, humpy, cute, sexy—all those adjectives would be fitting for his big-shouldered, narrow-waisted body. He had the flattest stomach in Christendom, was a little beetle browed and round nosed, and had that kind of

American quality of being taciturn and withdrawn that suggested he could fuck your brains out, given the chance.

C. C. brought him around in tow to see my new studio, an old church in Chelsea that I had been able to rent for not much money. But everything had to be done to it.

Henri Charles wrote me a note after he had been there and suggested himself as a renovator. He could paint, build, replace windows, and do myriad odd jobs, he claimed. And in exchange just wanted to be housed and fed. He could live in one of the back rooms at the church, it was true. There was a toilet and some pathetic attempts at heat already in place. I had to go back to the United States to complete some portraits and gather my things. I felt a strong undertow of physicality for Henri Charles, but the really major difference in our ages forced me to put aside any of those feelings.

I told him before I left that I didn't really expect him to complete such a major job by himself and that if the London winter and being alone got too much for him he was to abandon the project and I would think none the worse of him.

He turned out to be a trouper and when I returned had managed to seal the windows and get a coat of paint on the enormous space, repairing the broken plaster as he went. His spirits seemed good and he appeared to enjoy being with me. I also quickly became his confidant.

For his age he had a slept around quite a bit on both sides of the fence. Had almost gotten married in the United States in Seattle before departing for Europe. He had a short but violent affair with the man he had first stayed with in London but did not seem dismayed at its failure.

There was a poetic and magical side to Henri Charles. He had changed his own name from Henry to Henri shortly after leaving high school. Because he hated being called Hank.

Such silly things make us fall in love with someone. I was well on guard until the day he was on a ladder repairing some electrical wiring. As he raised his arms his sweatshirt pulled up, his pants sagged, and there was that wonderful taut stomach, muscles reaching down to his groin, reaching up to mold around his lower ribs. Something plunged inside of me.

It was very cold in London that winter and I suggested that he come use the extra bedroom in my flat in Knightsbridge when he caught a bad cold. He got over the cold and stayed in the room. Now we were spending all our time together. Working on the studio space, sharing meals, saying good night. How did we start giving each other massages? It really wasn't entirely my idea. I think he made it clear that he would enjoy it. They became semisexual rituals.

At best, Henri Charles was reeling me into the labyrinth of his sexuality unconsciously. At worst, he was deliberately enslaving me so as to ensure some security in London.

We spent weekends in the countryside visiting stately homes since it interested both of us. Knole was the major experience. Wandering through all those spectral rooms where the presence of strong but unknown personalities lingered. All of my aristocratic pretensions came to the fore. Henri Charles was moving as fast as he could away from Sandusky, Ohio, yet he wasn't really an *arriviste*. Even now I don't think he was trying to "make it"—he was trying to survive. And I do think he had a strong attachment to me there for awhile. Later he claimed that he never thought of it as a homosexual attachment, although that seems hard to imagine, since he had already slogged it to plenty of guys at that point in his life.

He saw young women while he was living with me, all of them plain brown hens to his muscular splendor. He had something of the French concept of the *baise de santé* in his makeup. He felt he had to have intercourse with someone just to stay on an even keel. But it wasn't going to be with me.

Isn't this a sad little story? I found it hard to imagine that it was happening to me. I had seen so many friends obsessed with young men. It was so unflattering to both parties. I had never been interested in anyone whose age was much different from mine. Was it a panicky grasping for fading youth? Was the mystery of Henri Charles a mixture of magical youth and sturdy male sexiness? Beats me, lieutenant. But it was awful when he left me.

He suddenly ran off to the continent with some American friends passing through. I got it into my head that he had AIDS and had gone somewhere to die. I wasn't at all myself. I felt like someone in a chapter by Proust. Talk about distorted behavior.

I was feeling faint in the streets. Calling everyone he might possibly know in London and in the States to see if they had heard from him.

Through C. C. I found him working in a restaurant in Greece. He became friendlier during my frequent calls to the restaurant and agreed to see me when he came back on a quick visit to London.

I was just lucky that it didn't work out even worse than it did. My close friends in London knew that I was in quite a state over Henri Charles, but I managed to keep painting, and in all honesty my work was neither worse nor better for all the emotional upheaval. Art is like a submarine plying its way deep below the surface, ignoring the storms or sunny calms on the surface of the sea. It was supportive for me to realize that all my teenage sobbing and hysterical and uncontrollable behavior was only a part of my personality. It wasn't all of it. But it was ugly. I was deeply ashamed of myself, but obsession is obsession. It was particularly awful in London, where good manners and calm behavior reign. No one was ever more of an "aging poof" than I was. I could hardly blame Henri Charles for finding me disgusting.

C. C. and other friends were true blue through the whole ugly mess. Which finally worked itself out. Henri Charles came back to London in the autumn. Finished the studio, which I had just left as it was, painting amid the half-full paint cans and unfinished floors.

Then suddenly Henri Charles got that motion picture industry job that he had originally come over for. There had been reorganizations back in Hollywood. Whoever had wanted him in London in the first place regained power and the job was his. I gave him the deposit money to get an apartment of his own and soon I was the worst person he had ever known.

Before I left London, Henri Charles and I had reconciled as friends. He sorted himself out emotionally and after a couple of false starts at creating a home with different men he now is well established with a good-looking Frenchman a few years younger than himself.

There has been no one important in my life since Henri Charles. I occasionally find someone not too much younger than myself who seems to be able to hold my attention mentally and sexually, but I can't really make the effort to cinch the deal. Now I'm back in New York where the streets are full of young men searching for some kind of arrangement while they launch themselves in acting careers. But it's all pretty obvious. Once you lose the ability to delude yourself about the nature of relationships, it's difficult to have one. You have to be careful.

Sophistication has been defined as "that period between disillusion and defeat." By those standards I'm still not a sophisticated person. I'm still a person Fred would easily recognize, both physically and emotionally.

Sexual Synopsis

Shortly after I moved back to New York from London, I had the opportunity to be in San Diego. An acquaintance of my London friend C. C. lived there and wanted a portrait. At C. C.'s recommendation of course.

I flew into San Diego and arrived much too early for my appointment. It occurred to me to go over to North Island and see if the apartment where I had lived as a young naval officer still stood.

Now there is a sweeping bridge over to the island, where the great naval base edges one end and a splendid Victorian hotel still stands where they filmed *Some Like It Hot.*

When Fred came to visit me on North Island we had gone back and forth on the car-carrying ferry that plied the bay between downtown San Diego and the island. We were aboard one night when we noticed that instead of arriving on the island we were heading down the channel. La Jolla was on the right. We were going out to sea. We were thrilled and thought perhaps the captain was drunk and we would wind up on one of the islands that stood offshore. Perhaps the captain was only having fun, or a deckhand snatched the wheel from his hands. Because soon we were curving back and depositing the passengers and cars on the usual dock.

I thought, too, as I drove over the bridge of the night when I had sensed Fred was arriving on the ferry and had walked down the street to meet him. Although there are any number of ways to walk to the ferry landing, I honed in exactly and met him in the dusk under an overhang of trees. We embraced, feeling we were all alone in the world. But I've told you all this. It was perhaps the most piercingly sharp "we should be together" moment of our joint lives. At least it was for me. Fred forgot those things promptly unless reminded.

Off the bridge I found the street where I had lived. I parked and walked up the narrow cement sidewalk. Everything was exactly the same.

The rectangular garden with the banana tree in front of the windows of the little apartment I had occupied was there. Two blockish buildings with Spanish tiles on their roofs and palm trees on the swath of grass between them still stood to the right. The wall separating the garden from the landlady's property was still there on the left. And so was she. There stood Mrs. McKay, still in one of those floppy, short-flowered muumuu-style garments she favored. Slightly hennaed hair still in a shapeless mop, like unsorted knitting, on her head. She looked across the wall and said hello, as though she knew exactly who I was. Still the gawky young naval officer who had occupied her rental flat thirty years earlier.

I looked down the garden to the open door of the apartment. I believed I could see the end of the green foldout sofa just inside the door. And the mushroom-colored wall-to-wall carpet. And a bit of the pecky-cypress wall paneling.

I felt a strong pull. And a sense that if I simply walked through the garden past the banana tree into the apartment I could simply shut the door behind me and I would be back there. Perhaps waiting for Fred to come from the beach. Perhaps waiting for a letter from him sent from Japan while he was in port there.

Even more recently I compiled an album of photographs of myself, from the age of nine months onward to the present. Not to show people, but to see if I could discern some growth, some pattern by looking back into my own eyes as the years flipped by.

The man who drops by to have sex (I don't think I can call him a lover) likes to look at this book as his body is surging on top of mine. I'm not quite sure why but I suspect to remind himself that this body he is plying with his own once looked like this . . . or this . . . or this. He is getting further and further through the book, each orgasm proceeding a few pages more. I have high hopes that one day before he stops screwing me he will reach the end and look down to see the true face instead of the photographed one. Perhaps that will be the day he climbs off and never comes back again.

Aside from all that, while compiling the photographs for my own personal history, I found one of Fred and me sitting in that little San Diego garden having breakfast. The girlfriend of the officer who lived across the street is seated with us, as well as a dark-haired, handsome young officer in uniform whom I only vaguely remember as visiting across the street. Fred is in the foreground turned toward the camera. He's wearing a very expensive cable-knitted cotton short-sleeved sweater, not a T-shirt exactly. The large bicep of the arm nearest the camera bulges out of the sweater sleeve. His tight, curly blond hair glitters in the sun. As I looked at this picture I could suddenly hear his voice. The accent that so precisely expressed his gentle nature. He is smiling and happy. Across from him I sit in a long-sleeved shirt with the sleeves rolled up. I'm cutting something on my plate and smiling at the camera too. Something in my upright posture suggests that I am less sexually giving than I actually was. Lush plants surround us, the banana tree spreads behind us.

Those days seemed to still exist when I revisited that apartment. And made me long to go back inside that apartment. Shut the door and open the daybed, waiting for Fred to return. I would take off all my clothes and put on a striped cotton bathrobe. Lie down on the bed and read with a little bedside lamp switched on.

Perhaps I would read a book that I found among all the other faded novels that were on the long bookshelf above the bed. It was a novel about navy buddies who often on their shore leaves would take two whores to the same bedroom and lying side by side on the bed make love to these two faceless women beneath them. Sometimes grasping each other's hands as they had their orgasms simultaneously, which they tried to do. Practiced doing. Finally became quite adept at doing, talking to each other to have a climax at the same time, one urging the other to hurry or to slow down.

After the navy these two men find themselves in the same town. The man the protagonist loves has married and comes to his old navy friend frequently to discuss the ups and downs of his married life, particularly the sexual aspects. The voice of the novel is a professor, unmarried, finally coming to realize that he loves the handsome, athletic, less intellectual friend he has known since their navy days. When he finally tells his friend, the other man seizes an andiron from the fireplace and batters him in the head, then leaves. The professor realizes that the handsome lover became violent at the realization that their love did exist. And that he did want to have sex with another man.

I was very surprised when I first read this book. As with many homosexuals, I felt that what had happened between Fred and me was quite rare. I was very aware that there were a good many homosexuals lurking about in the navy and in the streets of cities where I had been. But I guess I thought that was mostly about sucking and fucking. Not about falling in love.

This book put a kind of seal of approval on my love for Fred. Other men had felt the same things, had tried to act upon them. And had failed. Fred and I hadn't failed.

Then Fred would come in. I would put my book down. He would want to take a shower. While he started his shower I would pull the draperies across the window. Drop my robe and get into the shower with him. He would get erect and place his soapy cock between my legs. I would struggle to hold him as close as I possibly could as the hot water beat down upon us. We would fall to the floor of the narrow shower stall, trying to force our bodies onto and into each other so that we could become one. Fred would mutter, "This isn't working" and drag me out, dry us both off.

He would lie on his back and I would lie on top of him. We would kiss and then I would move down, licking his body. I loved to run my tongue over his chest and linger on his nipples. He was my only lover who was excited by having my mouth on his nipples. I became expert at sloshing back and forth between the two of them.

I would move down and wet his abdomen with my tongue and eventually reach his crotch. Our sex play wasn't all that advanced at that point and I would lick around the base of his penis. Perhaps I had never had it in my mouth yet, and that day I would slip it in.

He would pull me off and up to his lips, where he would kiss me while turning me over on the bed. He would enter me from behind, turning my head to one side so he could kiss me while his body moved in and out.

Later while he held me he would say, "You almost killed me this time, I got so excited."

This is what I thought as I looked at the open door into my old apartment. And then turned away to go back to my car. It was time to keep my appointment with the lady who wanted her portrait painted.

While driving there I thought about the joy I had had in my love for Fred that I hadn't ever had again. Other things, yes. But not joy.

But joy isn't something I ordinarily associate with intercourse. With Fred I think there was always something of being touched by the gods. Of course, it was a dream come true. I had imagined that one day my hero would arrive. And he did. In the guise of the young Apollo.

Fred looked like one of those ceiling paintings by Tiepolo. All smooth limbs and unconscious grace; even, open features with blue eyes and a crown of blond curls.

After we went to New York I became ever less conscious of how godlike he was, and our life was increasingly on two tracks. On one hand, Fred was wanting to end the sexual side of our relationship. On the other hand, exploring ever more inventively when we did have sex. You can fault me for undervaluing what I had but you can also give me credit for not wanting to haul around with me the guilt of luring Fred into sex he wanted to avoid. The conflict was his. The sorting it out was mine.

Fred always said that it was easy for him to forget about having sex, and that he had to be aroused and goaded into it by someone else. I wonder if it has slowly disappeared from his life. I wonder if he ever leafs back through the pages in his head and remembers my warm body underneath him while he's on top of his wife. Or perhaps there have been other women. Perhaps there have been other men. I so doubt that about slow-to-act Fred.

So that was my life with the Handsomest Man in the World. He made me feel loved. He made me feel complete. He made me feel I was capable of anything as far as love was concerned.

And then, as the gods do, he moved on. There would have been no holding him. And would I want to meet him now? That beautiful body thickened with age, and perhaps that salty, funny mind of his thickened, too.

Of all my lovers, he was undoubtedly the one who most deserved to be loved. And who was the most capable of loving. What more can I say about you, Fred my darling, than that?

The Last Word

I have the fantasy that finally one day Fred will return. He's heavier but in that solid way. In bed he says, "You feel good. It's been a long time." I say, "It's been a lifetime." And we laugh and laugh, clinging together in bed.

ABOUT THE AUTHOR

David Leddick was born in Montague, Michigan, and attended the University of Michigan, graduating with a degree in english literature. Before he began to write at age sixty-five, he was an officer in the United States Navy, a dancer trained in classical ballet, a director of television commercials, and an advertising executive. He has published three novels (*My Worst Date, The Sex Squad,* and *Never Eat In*) and numerous books on photography. He recently returned to the stage as the star of his own cabaret show. He divides his time between Miami Beach and France.

THE HANDSOMEST MAN IN THE WORLD

_____in softbound at $13.46 (regularly $17.95) (ISBN: 1-56023-458-X)

Or order online and use special offer code HEC25 in the shopping cart.

COST OF BOOKS_____

OUTSIDE US/CANADA/
MEXICO: ADD 20%_____

POSTAGE & HANDLING_____
(US: $5.00 for first book & $2.00
for each additional book)
(Outside US: $6.00 for first book
& $2.00 for each additional book)

SUBTOTAL_____

IN CANADA: ADD 7% GST_____

STATE TAX_____
(NY, OH, MN, CA, IN, & SD residents,
add appropriate local sales tax)

FINAL TOTAL_____
(If paying in Canadian funds,
convert using the current
exchange rate, UNESCO
coupons welcome)

☐ **BILL ME LATER:** ($5 service charge will be added)
(Bill-me option is good on US/Canada/Mexico orders only;
not good to jobbers, wholesalers, or subscription agencies.)

☐ Check here if billing address is different from
shipping address and attach purchase order and
billing address information.

Signature_____

☐ **PAYMENT ENCLOSED: $**_____

☐ **PLEASE CHARGE TO MY CREDIT CARD.**

☐ Visa ☐ MasterCard ☐ AmEx ☐ Discover
☐ Diner's Club ☐ Eurocard ☐ JCB

Account # _____

Exp. Date_____

Signature_____

Prices in US dollars and subject to change without notice.

NAME_____

INSTITUTION_____

ADDRESS_____

CITY_____

STATE/ZIP_____

COUNTRY_____ COUNTY (NY residents only)_____

TEL_____ FAX_____

E-MAIL_____

May we use your e-mail address for confirmations and other types of information? ☐ Yes ☐ No
We appreciate receiving your e-mail address and fax number. Haworth would like to e-mail or fax special
discount offers to you, as a preferred customer. **We will never share, rent, or exchange your e-mail address
or fax number.** We regard such actions as an invasion of your privacy.

Order From Your Local Bookstore or Directly From
The Haworth Press, Inc.
10 Alice Street, Binghamton, New York 13904-1580 • USA
TELEPHONE: 1-800-HAWORTH (1-800-429-6784) / Outside US/Canada: (607) 722-5857
FAX: 1-800-895-0582 / Outside US/Canada: (607) 771-0012
E-mailto: orders@haworthpress.com
PLEASE PHOTOCOPY THIS FORM FOR YOUR PERSONAL USE.
http://www.HaworthPress.com

BOF03